Colors in the Earth

by

Michael Eckers

To the men and women
of the American Expeditionary Force.

Prologue
July 1918

The sky was still dark; reluctantly giving way to the faintest hint of approaching sunrise in the east, over the German lines. Dautin shook himself to ward off the gathering dew beginning to settle on his uniform. A single drop formed right in front of his eyes along the edge of his helmet; he watched it grow and fall. The glimmering stars above told of a clear day ahead with the promise of more of the damned heat. As he looked to his right, the trench was packed solid with soldiers. Each man knew what he was to do, though few had any real idea of what lay before him.

The dull bark of a distant artillery piece signaled the beginning of what most of these men would later call their entrance into hell. In a moment the air was full of the noise of a thousand cannon going off, their shells screaming overhead on the way to deliver death to the enemy. Men ducked down; the automatic response of those who've never experienced this before. The barrage would last a good half hour then begin to move away at two hundred yards per minute. It was behind this covering fire that they would advance, through that 'no man's land' lying between the trench systems of the two great armies facing each other. It was always the hope that enough of the German machine gun positions and barbed wire entanglements would be destroyed to allow the Americans to break through. Dautin had done this before, twice. It was still an awesome display to watch; again he was thankful he was not on the receiving end of it.

He took a moment to adjust his equipment; canvas web belt with suspenders that made the load more balanced, less awkward to carry. In addition to his pack he had two canteens, food rations for a couple of days, more than 200 rounds of ammunition, grenades, a pick for 'digging in' and his 1903 Springfield rifle; Dautin was carrying nearly 70 pounds of gear.

As the sky lightened, men looked over the top to observe the huge explosions; the view was like hundreds of volcanoes spewing dirt

1

and debris skyward, as if the very earth was vomiting up the men that dared to carve their own trench systems into her. Most of them believed, really believed, there would be no enemy left alive; it just wasn't possible. The murderous barrage began to move further away; whistles blew, voices shouting, "Over the top, men. Let's go. Death to the Huns."

As he climbed up the ladder Dautin could already hear the tat-tat-tat of the German machine guns opening up. Men began to fall at once, a few back down into the trench, on top of those trying to follow up and over. "This is going to be close", he thought as he began to run, pulling his head down a bit, like leaning into a heavy rain. But there would be no rain today...

Chapter 1
July 1916

"You're crazy, you know that? Why would you want to join the army when all of Europe is tearing itself apart in this war?" Earl was heaving the last of the sacks onto the bed of the truck, a brand new Federal that had arrived from Detroit a week earlier. He and Dautin had come with their grandfather, Isaiah, into Oakview for supplies. Not that it was a big town like Minneapolis to the north; maybe a few hundred people surrounded by miles of rolling hills, creeks and some of the best farmland around. Oakview had been the center of everything in the county since it was founded in 1855, barely three years after the Dakota Indians had sold the land and been moved further west to make room for setters in the soon to be State of Minnesota. Now it boasted a creamery, flour and feed mills, several shops and a three story hotel with its own restaurant inside. The town was also where the stage line had stopped, the railroads now ran and new automobile roads were being built.

The two boys were best friends, never mind that one was adopted and the other a natural son of the land owner. Dautin often mulled over the idea that this was part of what made America so different; in another place and time the two would never have worked together. He viewed the war in France as one that might, perhaps, take the power of the wealthy rulers and spread it among those who did the work. Background wasn't their only difference; it was not hard to tell they were from different parents. Dautin had that middle height, broad shouldered body with the light brown hair and blue eyes. Earl was taller, by a full six inches, and had black hair, dark eyes and was very lanky. They did share in their enjoyment of the outdoors and hard work; it was not difficult to get a good effort out of either of them.

Earl had been raised from a young age at the orphanage in Owatonna; the actual name was the State Public School for Dependent and Neglected Children. His father had died when Earl was not yet seven years old. His mother could not care for all

3

five kids; she had taken the youngest two with her back east somewhere. Earl and two brothers went to live in Owatonna. By the time Earl was sixteen both of his brothers had died of illness, though it didn't seem to Earl like they were at all mistreated; they had just gotten sick and died. It was right after his birthday, two years ago, that the Weldon's arranged for him to come up to their farm in Oakview to work and live until his adoption was finalized. Their own son, Dautin, was the same age and they could use an extra set of hands around the place. Grandpa Isaiah was getting too old to work, being almost 70 years old himself. His son, Jack, had taken over the operation of the farm when he returned from the Army. Jack had served in Cuba during the War back in 1898. When the work had become too much for them, Jack brought Earl on board. He had become one of the family, his contributions being vital to the farm.

"Well, anyhow, the crop's nearly in and father says he can take on another hand. He says the decision is mine to make, just like he and Grandpa both did. I was wondering if you'd like to join up with me? The way I see it, if we go in now, we'll have the training before the country really pitches in over there. We'll have a leg up on all the others that will form the armies America will send."

Earl shook his head. "How can you be so sure we'll get involved? President Wilson is trying hard to keep us neutral and out of the war."

"Neutral? We ship food and weapons to England; how long before Germany starts sinking our ships with their submarines? I wouldn't be surprised if the wheat we raise, and our livestock, don't end up feeding the Brits fighting in France and Belgium."

"You boys just about finished? I'm hungry and I'll bet your ma has something good just waiting at home to be eaten. I'd hate to think your dad will get it all. Besides, I'm almost tuckered out from jawing with everyone. Who'd figure the first dad-gum farm truck in Oakview would cause such a stir. Must be seven or eight people wanted to know about it." Isaiah still had a wit, a sense of humor that had served him well back in his own war, so very, very long ago. The Civil War had ended a bit over fifty years ago; he'd fought for the Union back in those awful, gory, deadly times. He often said the only good to come out of that war was his marriage to Gramma Beth. They had first met down in Georgia when Isaiah was part of Sherman's siege of Atlanta. She had nursed Isaiah

4

back to health when he'd been wounded; Beth even moved up to Oakview when Isaiah had come home to recuperate. After the war they had taken over the family farm when Isaiah's brother moved to Rochester. Gramma Beth had passed away just two years ago; her patience and that southern charm were still missed by everyone. Dautin's mother, Phebe especially missed the only other female on the place. Even with all the modern conveniences, life was still hard work for a farm wife. Cleaning up after four men, cooking, washing and such would be enough; there were also the chickens, the gardens, and other farm work besides. Jack had recognized her plight; he had rebuilt the kitchen after Gramma had passed, adding a new sink with a pump. No more need to bring water up from the spring; he'd even gotten an icebox, right inside here, to keep the cold foods so handy. Phebe especially loved the name of it, the "Alaska Star"; picturing ice covered mountains every time she opened the door. Come winter, she planned on using it as more of a larder since the porch and mud room would keep things cold and had much more space.

"Hey Grandpa, what do you think of Dautin joining the Army?" Earl knew this question, or any question, would make for a nice story on the drive back to the farm.

"Well now, as I recall back in '62 it was more a notion of adventure for some of us. Will Grayson and I; you remember Will, don't you Dautin? Will and I joined as replacements, kind of like all those who will come later, like Dautin is talking about. There were times when I wished I'd been older and could've gone in right at the start. By the time I showed up, those early guys were all wearing stripes and life was a little easier for them. I don't mean the shootin' and fightin'; that's never easy for anybody. Life in camp was just a little easier when you're a Corporal or Sergeant. If you joined up now and we get into a shooting war with the Kaiser soon, you'll have stripes for sure. You'd be one telling the new guys what to do. I see the sense in that; this war's swallowing up soldiers by the thousands over there. I figure when we get involved, almost everybody will have to go anyhow. Shoot, with this Pancho Villa scoundrel and the fuss he's making down in Mexico, we might find ourselves in a real war before we even get into it with the huns. I guess you might as well get that leg up on 'em."

5

The rest of the drive home was so quiet, so full of thought, that Grandpa Isaiah took a nap.

Chapter 2
July 1916

Jack Weldon stared out the window at the field stretching down to the creek at the edge of he woods. The scene was so peaceful, so serene; the very essence of it soaked into his soul. Jack was not a man given to such a moment of inactivity and reflection. The memories of his life unfolded before him as the chapters of a book. His youth, spent on this farm, in this very kitchen, working the soil alongside his father. The years of violence that followed, years of fighting; first against the Indians out west, then the Spaniards in Cuba. Home again, grown up and responsible for a new wife and son. It has been a good life, one he would have done few things to change.

The sound of tires crunching on the gravel drive leading to the house snapped him back to the present; he thought how much quieter they were than the wooden wheels of a wagon. Jack turned, his mind already focused on what was to be done with the supplies that should be in the back of the truck. He was thankful for the moment of reflection, though it had caught him by surprise; back to the real business at hand now.

"Dad, boys, were you able to get everything we need?"

"Yes, sir." Dautin answered, as he set a box of foodstuffs for the house on the porch step. "We got every single thing on Mother's list, and all the supplies you told us about as well. Mr Fedder said we nearly cleaned him out of the wire fencing, but will order more in case we need it soon. He'll remind the ice company that we need another delivery the end of the week."

"That's fine; I don't think we'll need more fencing, but it's good to know. I dug a few post holes while you were gone. I think we'll be finished with the new pen in a couple of days. Dad, you look a bit tired; did the boys wear you out with all their talk?"

Isaiah smiled as he got out of the truck. "You know, I'm pretty well rested up now. Ready to take on a post hole or two myself. Somehow I think those two give me more energy than they take; maybe bottle some up, like an elixir."

Phebe Weldon, Jack's wife, opened the screen door from the kitchen. "Boys, will you bring those things in here? I'd like to get everything put away before I start on supper."

"Yes, ma'am", said Earl, as he picked up a box. Jack got into the truck and began to back it over to the barn to begin unloading the rest of the supplies. Dautin grabbed another of the food boxes while Isaiah held the door open for him. As the young man stepped past, Isaiah said softly, "After supper is a good time to talk about important things, you know."

Dautin paused, looked at his grandfather and nodded.

Later that evening Dautin spoke with his parents; both voiced their support for his decision to join the army now, before the nation was dragged into the war raging in Europe. His father offered to accompany him on the trip up to Fort Snelling at the junction of the Minnesota and
Mississippi Rivers. The fort had been built before any other American presence existed in the area, nearly a century ago. It was now a large army base, having been expanded in size following the Spanish American War in 1898; the war Jack himself had been involved in. It would be several days before they could make the trip; there was still the new hog pen to complete and Jack would have to arrange for a hired hand to take Dautin's place.

Although the work around the farm occupied most of his time, Dautin found an afternoon to head into Oakview to say goodbye to several people he knew and had grown up with. While he was at the feed store, 'Old Man' Fedder got out of his chair to come over and shake his hand. He was the son of the man who first started the store when Oakview was founded. His son now owned it; the third generation that would one day pass it along to his own son who was one of Dautin's friends.

"Young Weldon, I remember the day like it was yesterday. That fancy officer, all shiny and clean, was in here trying to sign up boys to go fight the Rebs. Why he got your grand-dad and that

Will Grayson both. I don't think I was more than seven years old myself. I really wanted to go along with Isaiah, that's for sure. Until he come back a while later, all shot up and pale. His girl, Beth, sure was a lot better lookin'." The old man smiled; a few teeth still in his gums. Dautin knew he meant well; Mr Fedder and his grandparents had been good friends for many years. Mr Fedder was even a pallbearer for Grandma Beth's funeral.

"Yessir, them huns better just watch out; they're in for a peck of trouble with another Weldon joining the army. If you do half as good as your pa, and his pa... well, I reckin' you'll know what to do when you get into a fight. It sure must be in your blood."

Dautin shook his hand and accepted the rather feeble pat on the back. After saying goodbye to a few other friends, he headed back home; the eight mile walk was a good time for him to give serious thought about his decision. The way folks like Mr Fedder talked, it didn't seem like it would be too hard at all. As he compared their opinions to those of his dad and grandpa, he felt it would be a lot more difficult than most believed.

When he got home, his mother pulled him aside and handed him a small rolled up cloth tied with a leather lace. "There's not many things the army will let you bring along at first. When you get a bit more settled in we'll be sure to send you whatever we've got that you'll be needing. This will come in handy, though I ought to take a bit more time showing you how to sew a button or fix a tear. This is the sewing kit I gave your father when I first met him. He sure needed it then." Phebe said with a chuckle. "Someday you'll hear that story; best come from your father."

After dinner, Jack told Dautin there were some things his mother had to show him. The next few hours were spent learning to thread a needle and how to stitch up a hole, put on a button and sew on a patch. Dautin really didn't think it was hard at all, but he got tired of sticking himself in the finger with the needle. Even grandpa said it was "ever so important to never leave your 'housewife' behind". His dad told him that's what it's called; sort of like a seamstress that travels with you all the time.

The morning came when it was time to go. Dautin finished his chores early and helped Phebe fix breakfast for all of them. The new hired hand, Samuel, had started two days earlier and was already feeling at home sleeping in the temporary room they'd fixed up in the barn. He'd be more comfortable once he moved into the room with Earl. It made Dautin a bit sad to think of someone else sleeping in his bed tonight. He noticed his mother kept looking at him and wiped her eyes more than once. Dautin went up to her and gave her the biggest hug of his life; that's when she started crying. A minute or so later she was finished and said it was her right to cry at his leaving, but she knew he'd be fine. She was going to pray his way through the army, just like she had for his father.

An hour later they were pulling up to the train depot in Oakview. The big locomotive was sitting on the track, steam issuing from a dozen small places beneath it as it slowly let out a "ssshhhuuuffff" through its stack on top every so often. A brakeman was working his way around, peering intently at connections and wheels. Another man with a long snouted oilcan in his hand was doing the same, except now and again he'd stick that snout into a spot and press down hard with his thumb, shooting oil into some strategic place. The boys went up to the depot window and purchased the tickets to Minneapolis. Dautin and his father would take a streetcar from there out along the Mississippi River to Fort Snelling, only a few miles away. He was looking forward to the ride up, spending time talking with Jack. He'd be checking in at the Fort before nightfall.

"You take care of yourself, brother. I don't want to go traipsing around the country looking to rescue you from some sort of trouble." Earl was joking to hide the sadness he felt at Dautin's leaving. Life on the farm would be very different from now on.

"Aww, you know you've wanted the bottom bunk to sleep on for quite some time. Anyway, if the war does start soon, I'm sure you'll be following me along. When we meet up, and I'm wearing stripes on my arm, then you'll HAVE to show me some respect." Dautin's grin was infectious and the three had a good laugh. With that, Jack and Dautin boarded the train and Earl waved goodbye.

The train ride was unforgettable for Dautin as his father began to tell him of the experiences he lived through during his own years in the army. Many of the stories were new; Jack had never shared much of what he'd done fighting Indians and the Spanish. Dautin had grown up hearing Grandpa Isaiah tell of the battles down south, but this was mostly new to him. He listened with rapt

10

attention as his father told of fatigue, hunger and death he'd seen in his years serving the country.

"You know, son, I'm not telling you these things to frighten you or change your mind. What you're doing is about the best thing possible. Without men like you and the Weldons before, this country couldn't go on as it is. Now it looks like America may be the only way to save what freedom is left in Europe; what we do there will go far in defending our own soil right here in Minnesota. If the Kaiser and his henchmen can beat the French and British, nothing will keep him from taking that step over the Atlantic and hitting us one day. I just know we'll be in it eventually; even President Wilson can see that. Our nation is getting ready; he's just buying us the time we need to better prepare for the coming fight. You're going to be a big part in that preparation; you'll be one of the leaders when the shooting finally starts. Listen to your officers and follow the lead of your Sergeants. They are the real deal."

After a few minutes of quiet reflection, Dautin spoke up. "Say dad, mother mentioned giving you a sewing kit when she first met you. She said the story had best come from you, but I don't know why."

"She did, eh? Well, it was like this. I had come home for a few weeks before heading down to Cuba. I wanted to see the family… well, you know, just in case. Anyhow, I heard there was a new teacher at the school and that she was real pretty to boot. I put on my cleanest uniform, saddled our best mare and rode over to introduce myself. Seeing as I was the only soldier around, I figured she would take to me right away. I rode up to the school while the kids were all playing outside. Well, the fuss I caused, being in uniform and all. The kids were crowding around when she walked up, prettier than I'd been told. I did my best dismount, had that leg way up in the air swinging over the rump of that mare; I guess maybe too high up. I heard a rip and when I got on the ground, my britches were split from belt to buckle, all the way from front to back. All I could do was get back on that horse and ride home as fast as she'd go. The next day, your mother came by with a sewing kit and taught me how to stitch up my trousers… just like she taught you."

Dautin could not remember ever laughing so hard or long.

11

Chapter 3
October 1916

Fort Snelling

"Ya know, Doc, I'm a thinkin' we're probably the only danged Regular unit that ain't down south on the Rio Grande sunnin' ourselves and learnin' to speak Mexican. Corporal Atherton was sayin' he read that the whole National Guard, all of 'em, are being sent down there by President Wilson. How come, if he's so against us gettin' into a war in Europe, we have to be fightin' the danged bandits down there?"

Dautin, now 'Doc' to most of the other guys, wasn't too sure himself about that one. It seemed that all he read about lately in the newspapers was how Pancho Villa was running circles around the Army. No matter how many units went down there, nobody could catch up with the banditos. Now he'd read that someone in Hollywood was making a movie about Villa, showing him to be some sort of hero; it all seemed really screwy to him.

"I don't know, Digger. I suppose it could be that Wilson figures it's a way to get our boys some training before we have to head across the Atlantic. General Pershing has command of more troops down there than we had against the Spaniards in Cuba. It's the largest group the Army's seen under one general since the Civil War. All for a bunch of two bit thieves; I'm just glad we're not down there. I don't much care for sand in my soup."

"All right you two... shut your yaps and get into those potatoes. There'll be hell to pay if you're not finished when Cookie gets back. He doesn't like having to explain that chow's late on account of a couple of rookies that don't know how to peel spuds." Corporal Atherton was the assistant to the company cook. Dautin and Digger were his assigned help for the day; the rest of the company was out at the rifle range for the afternoon. It was a cool autumn day and Dautin could smell the crispness in the air, even over the musty odor of the ton of potatoes he was surrounded by.

He was glad he'd pulled kitchen duty today; tomorrow there were some French officers arriving who would begin showing the company what the fighting was like over in Europe. Not that trench warfare was new to Dautin; Grandpa Isaiah had often told him of the times in the dirt against the rebels on the way to Atlanta. And as much as he enjoyed the practice at the rifle range, he was already the best marksman in the company; at least that's what he was told by First Sergeant O'Toole. The Sergeant was always picking Dautin to demonstrate the best position to shoot from in a situation. He was genuinely impressed that Dautin could hit the target, dead center, from practically any pose; probably even from standing on his head.

The past few months at Fort Snelling had been fun for Dautin; hard work, to be sure. He had dropped about fifteen pounds off his already lean frame but, somehow, seemed bigger than before. He was stronger and could double-time with a full pack for a couple of miles before he got tired. Even Lieutenant Schilling commended him for his fighting ability; he seemed a natural with the bayonet and could wrestle a much bigger man to the ground in an instant. He had also earned the respect of the other guys in the platoon. Despite appearing to be a 'teacher's pet' or something, his genuine sincerity and devotion to the other men's welfare had garnered him their admiration and the nickname Doc. He just seemed to know when someone was hurting or needed something; on a hike he'd be the first to attend to a comrade falling out from exhaustion or foot blisters. Often he'd be helping another soldier when the medical orderly arrived. Dautin was even offered the chance to become an orderly; he said he had joined to fight and meant to do just that.

The only thing he missed, being at Fort Snelling, was the opportunity to see his family. He'd not been granted any leave yet, at least not for more than a day at a time. He had taken a day to walk through Minneapolis and was looking forward to having a chance to see the state capitol building in St Paul soon. Grandpa had told him how marvelous it was; a fitting tribute to the soldiers of his generation. Isaiah had been there for the dedication of the building and again when they moved all the battle flags into their new home. He had been the color bearer of the Second Minnesota Infantry for quite awhile and was given the honor of carrying it, again, as all the flags were flown in a parade through the city. Dautin remembered watching, as a small boy, and caught the proud looks of the other people lining the streets, including his own father.

All the thinking and memories made the afternoon fly by. Suddenly Dautin realized that he and Digger had disposed of enough of the potatoes to satisfy the Corporal. They were dismissed for two hours and reminded to be back to wash dishes after chow. As they were walking to their barracks to catch a little 'shut eye', one of their platoon mates ran up.

"Hey, Weldon, the Captain wants to see you in his office right away."

"What's this about, Frank? I haven't screwed up on anything I can think of..."

"Beats me; he sent me running to find you at the chow hall. I'm just glad I met you halfway. Now I've got time for a smoke before I head back. You got one on you, Digger?"

"Sure, and a match and a kick in the gut to start it, too. Here."

Dautin hurried ahead of the other two and turned in to the company offices. The Captain's orderly told him to have a seat. At the very moment he sat, the door opened and Captain Andrews came in; Dautin jumped to attention, nearly falling in the process.

"Take it easy, private. You got here quicker than I expected; though, from what I hear that shouldn't be a surprise. Come into my office."

Dautin followed him in and stood at attention in front of the desk. Captain Andrews walked around and sat down. He pulled a file out of a drawer and opened it on his desk.

"I'm glad for the opportunity to meet with you, Weldon. I've heard good things about your progress so far. Lieutenant Schilling and First Sergeant O'Toole have both come to me with a recommendation that you be promoted to Corporal. Now that caught my attention since you've only been here a short time. I've never known either of them to be so impressed about anyone else. With that said, I'd like to know if you'd be interested in a special assignment."

14

"Excuse me, sir. I've explained to others that I joined up for active service. I'd prefer not to become a medical orderly, sir."

"I have no idea what you're talking about, Weldon. I'm interested in knowing if you'd consider assisting a visiting French Major and his crew when they arrive tomorrow? They're here to instruct our company in trench warfare and will need a driver and a few others to help out. I'd like you to be in charge of the other enlisted men on that detail. I've been told Major LeBeau himself asked for you personally. May I ask how you'd know a French Major?"

"Sir, I don't know any French Major, or any Frenchman at all. This whole thing is a puzzle to me, Captain."

"Hmmmmm, I suppose, Weldon, we will have to wait another day for the mystery to be solved. At any rate, the position requires a non-commissioned officer's rank. I don't know of any reason why I shouldn't follow the recommendations of my Lieutenant and First Sergeant. Congratulations, Corporal Weldon. Be sure to keep me informed of anything the Major will need while he's here, alright?"

"Yes, sir." Dautin snapped to attention and saluted. The Captain returned the salute with a smile and followed it with a handshake. Dautin turned, a bit dazed, and hurried out of the office. The orderly outside handed him a copy of his new orders and reminded him to have his stripes sewn on right away. Major LeBeau would arrive at 0700 tomorrow and Dautin was to meet him then at the Colonel's office.

When he returned to the barracks, Sergeant O'Toole was the first to come up and congratulate him. Several of the others in the company wanted to take him out to celebrate, but Dautin declined; he had to get busy sewing on his new stripes. He'd have to remember to thank his mother for teaching him how to do that.

The next morning Dautin reported to the office of the regimental commander, Colonel Stratton. It was a warm morning as the sun began its climb skyward; a few clouds drifted up high and a huge formation of geese was flying south. The birds were so far up they could not even be heard from the ground. Dautin wondered if there were still birds migrating above the battlefields of France. He'd have to ask Major LeBeau that question, if the opportunity arose. The Colonel's adjutant knocked on Stratton's door, opened it a bit and announced Corporal Weldon's arrival. He motioned for Dautin to step inside; in the office stood the Colonel, two French officers and Dautin's father!

"Ah, the younger Weldon I've been hearing about. No surprise really, I suppose. Major LeBeau, may I introduce you to Corporal Weldon, Jack's son."

"*Mon Dieu, il ressemble exactement comme vous avez utilisé.* Jaques, the boy, he ees you, so long ago."

"You know, I've never really noticed before; you're right. Now that he's filled out a bit there is quite the resemblance. How are you, son? I see you've gotten the first stripes already, eh?"

"I'm fine, dad; having a great time. I've even perfected the art of peeling potatoes. Mother's training is finally paying off. It's a surprise to see you here."

Major LeBeau's adjutant, Lieutenant Monier, translated Dautin's reply. The Major had a sad smile on his face as he spoke in a halting voice. "My own son, Peetare, he would be, ahhh, ayeteen years. The Boche ended hees life at Fort Douaumont in Verdun last spreeng."

Colonel Stratton put his hand on LeBeau's shoulder as he said, "I'm so sorry. I remember the day you first heard of his birth when we were in Santiago." There was a brief moment of silence, not awkward, more one of insightful thought. Stratton walked over to his desk and opened a box on it.

"Aaahh, Cuba. Hot and muggy, blisters and buggy; there was action enough to go around in those jungles." Colonel Stratton offered cigars to LeBeau and Jack. Dautin had never known his father to even think about 'lighting up'. This was like a different world to him.

"I remember when the three of us convinced Winston he should try the local tobacco. The look on his face as he watched that young girl rolling it on her bare thigh..." Jack glanced at Dautin, saw the raised eyebrows, and continued. "Sorry, son, haven't told you everything I did in the army. Now that young kid, fresh out of Sandhurst, in his starched wool with the equally starched manner, is the First Lord of the Admiralty for the King of England."

16

"*Oui, certainement.* Yes, and heee steel ees a, how ees eet? Ahh, an ass."

Jack looked at Dautin again. "I'll fill you in over a bite of lunch. Right now, I'm afraid you have some actual army business to attend to. This cigar is a good one, Colonel; it's going right to my head."

"Jack, why don't you take a few minutes now with your son? You know LeBeau; once they get started, it may be days before the Corporal has time to see anyone."

"Thanks, Tom. I'll have him back soon. Maybe breakfast will taste better than lunch anyway. We'll be back in an hour or so." With that, Jack and Dautin left the others talking about old times against the Spaniards in Cuba.

With breakfast in them, the two Weldons sat on a patio in the mid morning sunshine. Dautin was relishing the feeling of food that wasn't served out of a five gallon pot for a change. His father was explaining why he was here and who Major LeBeau was.

"So you see, Stratton and I were together when we shipped over to Cuba. We'd fought side by side against the Indians in the Northwest before that was all done. We met up again down in Tampa, Florida as the Army was preparing to go over to fight the Spaniards. We were assigned to ride herd on a bunch of foreign military officers going along as observers. The Major was a young Lieutenant then and Winston Churchill was a new officer fresh from Britain's West Point, their military school. I guess we ruined him for good when we taught him to smoke cigars. I hear he's hooked on them now. You never know who you'll meet in life or when you may run into them again later. In fact, I didn't even know where Tom Stratton was until the day you and I came up here. I met him as I was leaving; he asked if I'd be willing to show LeBeau around a little before his work here began. Well, as soon as LeBeau heard me talk about you being here and all he insisted you be part of his work; wouldn't have it any other way, really. Neither would I; you can learn quite a bit from him. That man is about the best the French army has. If he cared anything about politics, he'd undoubtedly have made general by now. Of course you'll have to work around his use of our language." Jack leaned back and smiled, remembering some other incident from years past.

17

"Dad, do you have any regrets about leaving the Army when you did? I mean, have you ever thought of joining up again?"

"Now? Absolutely not! There was a time when my decision to get out bothered me a little. Then I'd look at your mother, and you, and know with all certainty I'd made the right choice. Each of us must choose, at some point. I mean, well, you'll know someday whether this job is for one hitch, or two; ten or thirty years. Make the decision and don't look back. Indecision is what tears people up, and apart. I'm the happiest man I know."

Chapter 4
April 1917

Fort Snelling

The snow was falling in huge flakes that seemed like they might hurt if they hit you. Doc was leaning against his locker, looking out the barracks window near his bunk, feeling tired and a little frustrated. Everyone was a bit on edge; the weather didn't help at all. There was a feeling like a bug was slowly crawling up his back, tickling the skin but you knew it would soon stop and bite. Doc wasn't the only one who felt it; several of the guys had been saying something was going to happen.

The past months had been so busy none of the men in this barracks remembered the last time they had this much time off. All day they had been told to wait out the snow; that when it was through, they'd have plenty of opportunity to be out in it, getting the trenches shoveled out. They had spent the first two weeks of November learning how to dig. Now they all figured it was something they were pretty good at. After all, wasn't the Army known for keeping a man busy digging a hole and filling it back in? These trenches were different; eight feet deep, three feet wide and they zigged and zagged every five yards. Once they were dug, firing steps were built along with dugouts in the side walls for sleeping. Major LeBeau had been emphatic about the precision each was dug with. Then there were the communications trenches connecting the main lines and machine gun dugouts. The whole thing was a huge puzzle when you were on the ground; almost like a rat's maze. Then Doc was shown what they looked like from the air; a photograph had been sent over by the Signal Corps so his squad could see what they had begun.

The rest of November and all of December were a blur with the squad teaching other units from the various companies how to do what they had learned; to dig like never before. Soon the parade grounds and even the officers' polo fields were crisscrossed with trenches. Major LeBeau seemed disposed to grumble in his barely audible way that it would just have to do. Not nearly as pretty as those the *poilu* of the French Army could dig. Doc once asked the Major why his soldiers were called this; Digger had found out the word meant "hairy one". Major LeBeau grinned, pulled on the ends of his own enormous mustache and exclaimed, "*Mon Dieu, un français n'est plus de sa moustache.*" Lieutenant Monier tried to say that in France a man was a man only if he had a hairy face. Doc smiled and wondered what the Major would think of American infantrymen being called "dogfaces".

Much of February and March had been spent out in the cold, living in the trenches. They were told it was to acclimate them to the real conditions they would face when they got to France; if they got there was what many were thinking. The United States broke off diplomatic relations with Germany back in January because of the Kaiser's decision to resume unrestricted submarine warfare. Nearly 200 merchant ships had since been sunk by the u-boats in the Atlantic, but America remained neutral.

Doc snapped back into the present when he heard voices whooping and hollering in the hallway outside the door. Opening it up, he spotted Digger laughing and thumping another soldier on the shoulder. "What in blazes is going on here?" Doc asked.

"President Wilson done declared War on Germany! We just got the news; hey, open the window. Somebody said you can hear the bells of the churches in town." Doc opened the window he had been watching the snow through and, sure enough, he heard the bells; their sound was a bit muffled by the snow. All he could think was how busy he'd be from now on; the past months would probably look like a walk in the park.

After all the talking, the threatening; Germany's on again and off again policy of unrestricted submarine warfare. What had finally caused the President to throw his hat in the ring was a telegram that the British had intercepted. Apparently Germany was trying to convince Mexico and Japan to start a war with the United States; the Kaiser was guaranteeing them most of the western and southern states once America had been beaten!

It seemed like the very next day trucks began to arrive, full of lumber to build dozens of new barracks and kitchens and storehouses. About two weeks later the tide of new recruits began showing up by the trainload. Doc was briefed along with several other Sergeants and Corporals about what was coming up; the new men would be issued whatever clothing was at hand and then instruction would begin. All of these civilians would be turned into soldiers quickly; by the time the snow was melted they would begin training in the trenches. He overheard one Captain saying the first Americans were expected to ship over to France by summer!

Doc read a copy of the Minneapolis Journal, the evening paper; it stated President Wilson had ordered that more than one million soldiers be ready to help France and England against Germany by the beginning of 1918. To many it seemed impossible; when Doc had joined up in the summer of '16 the whole army numbered less than 150,000. He was hoping to be among the first to step foot in Europe; the last job he wanted was to stay back here and train all those who would do the fighting.

As often happens in a Minnesota spring, the next day dawned clear and warm. All the snow of the past couple of days melted and the robins had a field day pulling the reluctant nightcrawlers out of the earth. Doc and the other soldiers did not enjoy their afternoon nearly as much. Working out on the trenches in ankle deep mud that sucked your shoes off was no one's idea of fun. Major LeBeau laughed at the spectacle of the doughboys slipping and falling in the goo; at one point he turned to Doc and said *"Parfait. La boue uniformes de couleur."* Doc smiled and guessed what he was saying. "Yes, sir, if we have to fight in the mud, at least the Huns won't be able to see us; our uniforms are about the right color."

Chapter 5
May 1917

As the train chugged into the town of Oakview, Dautin was glad to see that Earl was there to pick him up. He had hoped the message he left on the phone call to Fedder's store had gotten out to the farm. A telephone was about the only thing they didn't have at home; maybe the wires would reach out there before too long. He hopped down off the bottom step and strode over to Earl; their smiles mirrored each other.

"Am I glad to see you. I've wanted to come up to Fort Snelling for some time now, just seems like there's one thing after another to do or fix or get ready for spring planting. Everyone's waiting for you; ma's got a special meal all set to go. We're having a ham off the first of the hogs we started last year. What with having to haul 'em to the locker here in Oakview and the cost to have them smoked, we figured we'd just build our own smokehouse. 'Course that means having to cut more wood, but Sam's getting really good at swinging an ax. He's fit in right from the start though he snores louder than you do."

"Well, I guess you'll have to put up with the both of us this week. I've got five days before I have to be back. Then we'll be heading out to New York to get ready for shipping over to France. I'm so glad to finally be going over; it's been almost a year since I left here and all the training and getting ready has made me downright hungry to see some real fighting. There's so few of us going right away, we don't figure on counting for much. We're just going to get things ready for the big show that will be coming after us. Word is they're planning on sending a quarter of a million men a month by late fall."

"I hope to be along with them, too. I've already let ma and pa know that I'll be signing up this summer if I'm not drafted first." Earl looked at Dautin with an expression that cried for approval.

"You just be sure to get yourself in my unit if you're joining the infantry. I'd hate to have to try to find you in an army of a million guys that all look the same! There are other kinds of service; cavalry, signal corps and such. Just don't join the Navy; we'd never forgive you for that!"

"Navy? I can't imagine being stuck on something floating on the ocean with the enemy shooting torpedoes at you from under the water where you can't even see him. No sir, it'll be infantry for me. I've already decided on that; now I'm just waiting for the right time to go. Looks like dad will have to take another trip down to the orphanage soon."

When they arrived at the farm, Dautin fairly ran to greet his mother and Grandpa Isaiah. He hadn't seen either of them since he left for Fort Snelling the previous summer. Hugs abounded with accompanying pats on the back and hearty handshakes. Phebe had outdone herself with the meal that followed. The ham was smoky, juicy and delicious. All the home canned vegetables Dautin could imagine were served in heaping amounts. Earl and Sam offered to clean up; Phebe was surprised and gratefully accepted the kindness. She walked with Jack and Dautin down to the creek where the three sat and talked about what Dautin thought the future might hold for himself. They returned after nearly an hour and found Grandpa Isaiah napping in his chair on the front porch in the warm spring breeze. Phebe went into the house and returned a few minutes later with a large tray; she served up warm apple pie with a thick slice of fresh cheese on top. Dautin felt like he could sleep for a week when he finished dessert. Grandpa Isaiah had other ideas; over steaming mugs of fresh coffee he pumped Dautin for all the stories he had from his time in service so far. When he tried to imitate Major LeBeau, Isaiah's face would contort before he bellowed with laughter. Watching Isaiah, Jack and Dautin share experiences with Earl and Sam listening in rapt attention, Phebe felt that strong surge of pride that all mothers feel for their men and boys. She quietly cleared the dessert dishes and was just beginning to wash them when she felt the strong arms of her husband slide around her waist. Turning to him, she received his thankful kiss and unspoken praise for her wonderful meal.

"Buttercup, you work so hard around here taking care of us. Let me do these dishes while you go and listen in on some of that "good old days" chatter out there. Lord knows you deserve to be off your feet for a rest more than any of us. I'll be catching up on Dautin's stories and I've heard all of dad's about a hundred times."

This was a trait she hoped Jack would pass along to the boys. She had fallen in love with him years before; not because of his bravery, which she never questioned. He had a heart full of gratitude and compassion that made her wonder, sometimes, how he had ever managed to fight so hard in war...

Dautin had a week to spend at home before he, and the rest of the regiment, departed for the long journey to France. The time passed quickly as he kept busy helping with the chores. He and Phebe even found an afternoon to go into the woods and came home with a big load of mushrooms; they were a favorite and only grew for a week or so before the ground dried up. Dautin visited the schoolhouse he'd attended and where his mother had been a teacher. He tried to imagine his father riding into the schoolyard, making a spectacle of himself as he split open his pants dismounting, trying to impress her. He made a point to visit friends, especially the Fedder family, before he returned to Fort Snelling.

Chapter 6
June 1917

Dear Mom and Dad,
Hope this letter gets to you before we sail to France. I'll try to remember and write all that has happened since we left Fort Snelling a few weeks ago. We've been so busy I'm exhausted most nights and just want to sleep instead of writing letters. I earned a two day pass and spent yesterday in New York City; about all I can say is that it's so big and crowded. I must have heard every language in the world spoken as we walked the streets. I also took in a baseball game at a place called the Polo Grounds. I got to see the New York Giants play against a team from Philadelphia. The way the Giants played, I wouldn't be surprised if they win it all this year. It was sure better than watching the Oakview Creamers play Northfield. They had running water in the ball park and you could get a beer and a "Coney dog" for five cents. A man came up and paid for Digger and me to get in, have lunch and everything. He said he'd fought against the Moros in the Philippines and got real excited when I said you'd been in Cuba. He was right proud to be able to buy a game and lunch for two boys who were so eager to go "beat the Hun".

We left Fort Snelling on special trolley cars to the main train station in Minneapolis, then loaded twelve cars with men and supplies. It was a straight ride to Chicago where we changed trains and rode all the way to the army camp at Plattsburg, New York. If I remember right, that's the town where great-great-grampa was during 1812 (I may be wrong on that). Anyway, the camp is a big one and has the officer school on it. I've never saluted so many people before!! We stayed at Plattsburg for about a week and since then have been housed near the big city here in a spot where they're building a huge army camp that will open later this summer. We've been practicing a bunch on identifying uniforms of the other armies we'll fight with, and against, soon. My French is getting better thanks to Lieutenant Monier; he's been teaching me a couple of hours each day right after noon chow. It seems I'm part of an advance unit that will be training regiments as they arrive in France. I hope my turn to fight doesn't get pushed back because of it. I've also been promoted (again) and now wear three stripes. Mom, your son can sew on stripes pretty quick now (though they are not as straight as you'd do). Don't know when we'll leave the good old USA but I feel it won't be long now.

I hope everything is okay at the farm with Earl and Sam doing my chores and all. Has Earl decided whether he will be joining up soon, too? Tell them to leave a few fish in the creek for when I come home again. I've included a new address for you to write a letter to me; it will be a good one to use while I'm in France, too.
Your loving son,
Dautin

Phebe put down the letter after reading it to the family and wiped away a tear. Jack cleared his throat and said, "Well it seems like he's doing well. The Polo Grounds; before I left for Cuba, all I saw was a busted down old country racetrack in Tampa. Of course, that was in Florida where there wasn't much but sand and scrub bushes. Even the hotel there was only for the senior officers! Dautin's having quite a time and I'm sure LeBeau will see him safely through whatever comes next. He's a fine man, the Major."

"New York City. Can't say as I'd like to see a place bigger than old Chicago. That was 'bout the biggest town in the world to me back in '62. Why I remember..."

Earl and Sam excused themselves at that; said they had all the evening chores to do before supper. Isaiah gave them a short, annoyed look and continued his story even as Phebe slowly backed out into the kitchen and Jack sighed, smiled and moved closer to his own dad.

Once in the kitchen Phebe stood, looking out the window down to the creek. She could almost see the young sandy haired boy running, chasing a grasshopper. She closed her eyes and seemed to hear his laughter as he caught one and headed to the house to show her. Wiping her eyes again, Phebe sat at the table in Dautin's spot, folded her hands and began to pray for him and the other boys preparing to go to war.

Chapter 7
June 1917

The ship pitched and rolled in the heavy swells. Dautin rolled out of his bunk and headed up the stairway (ladder to the crew) to get some fresh air. Digger was still in the berth below him, moaning when he wasn't throwing up in a bucket next to him. Many of the men were seasick; those that weren't ran the chance of puking at the sight and smell of the compartment they were housed in. In all there were nearly 100 men in a space that would be comfortable for no more than twenty.

On deck, Dautin was invigorated by the salty spray as the huge waves broke alongside the ship. He'd never been in so much as a boat on a lake. The other guys thought it was hilarious that someone from Minnesota had never been on water before. The most he'd ever done was to wade in a creek and fish in a river from the bank; and the Straight River was only about thirty feet across where it ran into the Cannon down near Faribault. Here he could see no horizon even, as the foamy gray spray melted into the same color as the clouds that scudded across the sky.

They'd been at sea for nearly a week and the wind and clouds had started yesterday. The ship's crew was pleased as this kind of rougher weather tended to keep the German submarines from attacking. They preferred cloudy days with a calmer surface to launch their torpedoes. Dautin thought he could stand being on the ship in waves like this forever if it kept the U-boats away. He had heard they could expect a ten day crossing; in these conditions it would certainly take a bit longer. If the weather cleared and the seas mellowed, the ship would make a fine target. It sailed alone and was relying on its relatively fast speed for safety.

Shortly after sunrise the next morning word traveled amongst the soldiers that the ship had passed through wreckage left from the sinking of another ship, perhaps only a couple of days earlier. Bodies in life jackets floated in the debris. The ship could not stop or even slow down; a German sub might be waiting for it to do just that. The mood of everyone aboard became somber and the sound of thousands of voices grew strangely quiet. The storm had eased somewhat but the sky remained the sullen gray it had been for most of the voyage. Later that afternoon the sound of the engines slowed and a shout came down below decks that land had been sighted and France was on the horizon. Hundreds of the doughboys scrambled to get on deck to try for a view of it. Dautin remained below, knowing he'd see plenty of France before he returned home.

Chapter 8
July 1917

The past few weeks had been an absolute whirlwind for Dautin and the rest of his squad. He was relieved to find Major LeBeau and Lieutenant Monier had arrived in France a week before the Americans; quarters were obtained for the doughboys at a former boarding school. It would be a fine arrangement with the entire unit together under one roof. The day after they had settled in their real work began; setting up all the varied training stations for the troops that would soon be flowing into the country from the United States. The location was near the town of Gondrecourt, nearly 100 miles north of Paris, due east of Calais and only 12 miles west of the Belgium border. The town would become known to hundreds of thousands of Americans as the place they learned about war. The front lines were a half dozen miles away; at times the shelling sounded like distant thunder. Not so many months before, this area had been behind the German lines.

Dautin now realized the actual scope of what was intended; his little group of twenty or so from Fort Snelling was one very small part of an immense facility to introduce the new troops to twentieth century warfare. Thousands of French colonial troops, mostly from Siam and Indochina were being used to build warehouses, barracks and the other necessary facilities. Before the flood of reinforcements arrived, hundreds of miles of rail lines and roadways needed to be laid, along with telephone wire for communication. Dautin overheard two officers talking about the expected arrival of telephone operators by the dozen; girls recruited in the States from French classes at various universities.

Soldiers arriving would barely know how to fire their weapons and maneuver as companies of a hundred or so. They would spend three to four weeks at this base getting their first real look at what trench fighting was about. It would include training in communication, artillery support, infiltration of enemy lines and a host of other subjects; there was also a sort of college for training up the officers. After this phase, each regiment would be

29

assigned to brigades and divisions and moved up into the front lines for a period of time. They would be alongside French and British units, continuing to 'show them the ropes'; helping them gain badly needed experience before the Yanks could operate as a separate American Army. It staggered Dautin's imagination to think of what it would take to build up that army to number between one and two million men. He wondered what it would look like to see that many men on the march, to feel the earth tremble under the cadence of their feet. As the thought of it staggered his own mind, he began to think of the fear it must be causing in the minds of their enemy.

"Well, sir, I figure the sooner we get after the Huns, the quicker I'll get back home. Besides, the unit will be better able to train the new troops if we have some real experience to back up what we show them."

"Like your fathair... queeck eento the war." Major LeBeau smiled at the earnest look on Dautin's face. "So, we try it tonight."

Lieutenant Monier showed up in the men's quarters an hour later. He explained that six of them would go with a French squad on a raid to capture some German prisoners. This was a common mission along the front lines; snatching a few of the enemy helped gather intelligence. A dozen or so would slip out of the trenches after dark and make their way through the barbed wire entanglements separating the opposing forces. With luck, they would surprise enemy lookouts and capture a few alive, bringing them back for interrogation. It was very dangerous work; Monier referred to it as "nasty beeznez".

Dautin, Digger and four other men were chosen for this first mission. They were motored east to within a mile or so of the French front line. As the evening sun dropped low in the sky behind them, the Americans made their way through a landscape very different than the France they had been staying in the past weeks. The ground was torn up everywhere, shell craters overlapping until there was no untouched earth remaining. Splintered tree trunks lay scattered about; chunks of concrete and bricks indicated the general area of a former farmhouse or other small building. They were reminded to stay low and to spread out a bit; groups of men attracted enemy artillery and mortar fire.

Suddenly the ground opened at their feet. They had reached the beginning of hundreds of miles of earthworks that would be their home for the months ahead. This was a traverse; a short trench running forward, connecting with the main parallel line ahead. As they entered the front line, with its firing steps and dugouts, Dautin was reminded of the system they had dug at Fort Snelling. He smiled at Digger, who nodded in agreement of the familiarity of the whole thing. They both sensed the excitement that this was different; this was the real deal.

Dautin realized that all the training, the anticipation had led to this moment. His desire to 'do his part' was about to run into the hard reality of war. He felt a tightening in his stomach; seemed to hear and see and smell sharper than ever before. As he reached up to adjust his helmet strap he felt the texture of the leather; how it differed from the colder brass of the buckle. In his mind he caught the briefest glimpse of his parents standing in front of their house before snapping back to the confines of the trench.

Lieutenant Monier introduced the men to a Sergeant with a huge, bushy moustache and a uniform crusted with mud. His eyes and a toothy smile seemed so bright in the dingy atmosphere of the trench. Dautin nodded to him and said, "Poilu."

"Oui, oui. Ami", came the gravelly response along with the firm grasp of a grimy hand. "Accueillir en France, la porte à l'enfer." Monier laughed and translated, "Sergeant Nopal welcomes you to the French entrance to hell. Let us hope the door does not shut behind us."

These French were men of the 47th Chasseurs Alpins, known as "The Blue Devils". Digger said he could have guessed at their nickname simply by the way they appeared. Sergeant Nopal spent the next hour preparing the Americans; removing excess equipment, helping them smear mud over hands and faces. He nodded his approval at how well the color of the mud matched their uniforms. His own was made of light blue trousers and a matching coat. The men stacked their 1903 Springfield rifles and were handed two pistols each. Their long bayonets were laid next to the rifles and trench knives were given to them as replacements. Each man was also given a half dozen grenades. One or two mumbled approval at the heft of these hand sized bombs that would shred a man with shrapnel in an instant. They were told to follow Sergeant Nopal and keep quiet; there would be time to talk when they came back.

Climbing and crawling out of the trench, Dautin found himself in a maze of craters and mounds of earth where each turn revealed terrain identical to what he'd just left. Gravel in the mud chafed knees and elbows as it worked its way into the wool of their uniforms. The group moved for, perhaps, a half hour before Nopal suddenly dropped out of sight a few feet ahead. Dautin practically fell into the German trench, barely able to keep his footing without making a racket. He saw two eyes and those teeth and knew Nopal was within inches of his face. "Shhhhh..."

A dim light shown ahead, faintly silhouetting the helmets of two enemy. Nopal motioned for Dautin to come with him, pulling his knife out of the sheath as he moved. Two other French soldiers then threw grenades beyond the two Huns and to the other end of the trench, effectively sealing off the approach of any more Germans. Nopal and Dautin were on the two sentries before they had a chance to react. With knives at their throats, they quickly dropped their rifles; shoulders slumped in surrender. The group retreated back out of the trench and made their way, as fast as they could crawl, back toward the French lines. German machine guns began firing; luckily off to their right. A flare popped overhead, illuminating everything in a stark, brilliant bluish white light. They only had a few yards to go when a mortar round landed behind Dautin. He heard the explosion and felt dirt rain down on him, along with the scream of one of the men. Turning, he headed back and found a French soldier writhing in pain and holding the stump of what had been his lower leg. Dautin immediately began to drag the man toward friendly lines ahead. He felt bullets tugging at his sleeve and one ricocheted off his helmet as he fell into the trench with the wounded poilu landing on top of him. Hands grabbed at him and lifted the other soldier off, quickly moving into a dugout to tend to him. Dautin stood up and was instantly engulfed in the embrace of Sergeant Nopal.

"L'héroïsme américain magnifique."

Digger and the other Yanks were, rather quietly, whooping it up in celebration of making it through their first fight. One of the Wisconsin boys, an inveterate scrounger, brought out a flask of bourbon and traded drinks of cognac with Lieutenant Monier, who was relieved to see them return safely. Dautin turned down the offer of a cigarette but accepted one quick swallow from the flask; the liquid burned his throat before filling his insides with a welcomed warmth. He had done it; had faced the enemy and not flinched or held back anything! He would remember every minute detail, none more than the eyes and teeth of Nopal in the Hun trench. This sense of heightened awareness dropped off and he felt relaxed ... and a bit tired.

The squad made their way back to their own quarters with increased confidence in their step. They talked amongst themselves about the raid; each confessing to the fear he had felt and how it was overcome. All agreed the training they provided others must include discussion on the reality of being afraid.

The next morning found Dautin in the office of an American Major. He and Lieutenant Monier had been summoned there by two rather large and armed soldiers. The Major looked none too pleased as he began to speak.

"So, Sergeant Weldon, I understand you went 'over the top' on a bit of an excursion yesterday; on whose authority, may I ask? You must be aware that the United States Army's position is that we are not yet ready to enter the fighting in this war. We've only arrived and until we're fully trained and organized, we are not to take an active role in the combat here. What have you to say?"

"Sir, although our unit is part of the First Division, we're directly commanded by Lieutenant Monier here and under the formal command of Major LeBeau. We obtained the Major's permission to accompany a French platoon, of "The Blue Devils", as part of our training. I believe that would be in accordance with directives."

"So you talked your way into a trench raid by going around the Division's own command system? Hmmm, looks like we may have some holes to patch up before others do the same. I want to make this very clear, Sergeant; you are not to do this again. Until we receive orders, from our own command, there will be no more trench raids or other adventures outside of your assigned duties as instructors here. Have I made myself clear, or would taking a stripe or two off of your sleeve be a better way to get through to you?"

"Perfectly clear, sir. Does the Major need me for anything else? I should be getting back to the squad we're running through the trenches this afternoon, for training, sir."

"No, no. That will be all.... oh, there is one more question, Sergeant. Would you be so kind as to write up a report on your adventure? I'd like to send it up the chain of command; it seems you may well have been the first of us to actually encounter the Huns. My personal congratulations, Weldon; but officially, I have to remind you there'll be no more of this."

"Yes, sir." Dautin and Lieutenant Monier saluted and turned to leave when the Major added that those who'd been on the raid were to be at Assembly the next morning in their best uniforms. It seemed a French General was going to present some medals...

Chapter 9
August 1917

The training facilities at Gondrecourt were filling with troops and activity. It seemed that more trains of '40 by 8's' were chugging into the station every day. The boxcars used to transport the soldiers were designed to hold 40 men or 8 horses; each was labeled as such. Dautin and Digger had heard that hundreds of Americans were arriving weekly at the French ports and making their way here and to a few other bases like this that were under construction. The plan was for the American army to grow by a quarter million men each month by the spring of 1918; it all seemed hard to believe. Dautin felt it would be impossible to find Earl if he ever did actually show up in a uniform.

The only mail he'd received from home, so far, had been a letter his folks had mailed while he was still in New York. He expected that mail would not be quite as high a priority on the ships as men and supplies; still, he was more than a little disappointed in not knowing what was going on back at home. Perhaps tomorrow there would be some news.

Their schedule had become a routine; reveille at 0500, breakfast for his unit followed quickly and then they were out on the field, running squads of fifty men at a time through drills in the trench systems. One day it might be about organizing and sending out a trench raid, their own specialty; another would be a mock gas attack. Dautin hated those; he felt the use of poison gases on an enemy was just wrong, no matter how effective it might be. The masks they used for protection were uncomfortable, unwieldy and didn't work on all the various types of chemicals thrown at them. Some of the new weapons showing up on the battlefields now included gas that caused a soldier's lungs to fill with his own body's fluids, drowning him. Others were blistering agents, like mustard gas, that stuck and caused chemical burns on your skin or in your lungs if you happened to breathe any in. These were horrible inventions that changed the whole complexity of fighting. The American Army was not as advanced in this new type of warfare, but was only beginning to develop its own chemicals and the systems needed to deliver them into and behind the German lines.

Two weeks earlier Dautin and Digger had visited a French hospital along with Major LeBeau and Lieutenant Monier. The visit was to show the effects of these new weapons. They had seen with their own eyes those soldiers who would suffer from the attacks. Some would recover in less time than from being shot; others were permanently blinded or would die slowly, struggling for air and coughing up blood. Both of the two young Americans were horrified by the visit; at the same time they left the hospital more determined than ever to do their part in seeing the war to an end.

"The Boche, they weel pay much for starting thees war. When we defeat them, there weel be leetle mercy." Major LeBeau had a serious and hateful look on his face as he spoke. Monier nodded in agreement. Dautin knew the personal rancor the Major held for the enemy, his own son having been killed earlier in the fighting. He had also been told by the Lieutenant of his loss; two brothers were now dead and his wife and newborn daughter had been killed in the shelling of their village up in the area known as Flanders, along the Dutch border. Often Digger and he discussed how they would feel in similar circumstances; Dautin would remember the stories he'd heard from his Grandma Beth about her home in Georgia during the Civil War and how devastated the areas around Atlanta had been. Both of them felt proud to help here in France and were so glad the fighting was not happening where their own families lived.

"You know", Digger started, "it's been a long time since I felt this mad toward people I've never even met. Don't really know if I ever have. What can make people do things like this to each other? Quite a few of my friends back home come from German families; I can't see them starting a war like this."

"Digger, I'm not sure I know the answer. Seems to me it's more like the country itself. This Kaiser is more than a king, I suppose. In my mind he has to be; England has a king and they don't seem as rotten as the Heinies. I think, maybe it's because the people don't have any say in their own lives. What I do know, deep inside, is that we've got to do all we can to stop any more of this kind of thing from happening. If it takes killing Germans, that's what I'll do. I do hope someone comes up with a better way; until

36

then I'm going to be seeing those boys in the hospital every time I shut my eyes until this is over."

Now the training schedules were condensed as more and more new troops began to arrive. For the first time Dautin and his squad were responsible for instructing Marines in the fundamentals of European warfare. Dautin appreciated their serious attitudes; it wasn't only the darker green of their uniforms that set them apart. When they marched it was with a precision that seemed a bit lacking in the Army. He and Digger were amused the first time one of them responded with "Aye Aye" when given an order. It seemed a little strange to think of hearing a form of 'sailor talk' out here in the middle of France. There was no doubting their dedication to the training and their oft spoken desire to get into real action against the Hun. These Marines were part of the new Second Division; it seemed the training of the First Division was complete. Dautin wondered when his squad would be replaced and head up to the front lines with the "Big Red One"; he hoped it would not be long.

"Hey Weldon, mail call. You finally got some from home", Digger called out as he was walking up. "Whaddayaknow, even I got two letters from the family."

Dautin gratefully took the stack of letters handed to him and found a shady spot beneath some large oak trees. It was already his favorite spot to rest in the afternoon and reminded him a bit of the farm back in Minnesota. As he looked at the postmarks on the letters to put them in order, he saw that one from Earl was mailed from New York. Not waiting, he opened it first.

New York City
July 7th

Hey "Doc",

Funny how I had to join the Army to find out your new nickname. The fellas up at Fort Snelling said to say hello; at least those who still remember you. I was there for only two weeks of processing and training. It seemed like we got haircuts, shots, pills, uniforms and then headed here to New York. I imagine this base looks different from when you came through. There must be close to 100,000 soldiers in barracks here. There are still more buildings going up every day and the noise is awful. We're not allowed to go into the City without a pass and they're pretty hard to get. I was hoping to see a baseball game like you did but I'm not sure that's going to work out.

Some of the guys in my company are from the area so we have plenty to talk about when we're not being TALKED TO by the Sergeants. They sure know lots of ways to make sure you hear them, most of them are loud and the language they use could peel paint off the barn! Hope I don't find out you talk that way since you got your stripes. I think we're shipping out in a couple of weeks; I'll probably be standing next to you by the time you get this. See you in France. Earl

Dautin spent most of the next hour reading through the other letters; several from his parents and Grandpa. There was one from a former school teacher and even Old Man Fedder had taken time to scribble a note of thanks and reminding him to "give it to the Kaiser"...

Chapter 10
September 1917

Dautin was disappointed he hadn't been able to locate Earl before his squad moved up to the front lines. He was hoping to share what he'd already learned about France and the fighting here. He knew that the training Earl was going to get wasn't going to be enough to really prepare him for what lay ahead. There just wasn't time; the American Army was growing faster and the French and British were getting anxious for the 'Yanks' to take over some of the ground. Everything pointed to real fighting when spring came around again. There was sure to be some sporadic raids, almost like two boxers sparring, before then. LeBeau, newly promoted to Colonel, had been sincere when he had his final talk with Dautin. The Colonel was now commanding a French regiment and wanted to tell his American comrades what he knew was happening. It was thought that the Russians were going to end their part in the War; that would allow Germany to transfer most of its eastern troops to the west. LeBeau felt that in 1918, when those Germans arrived, they would try to win the war against the Allies before the strength of the Americans became too great. He hoped the French and British could hold on until summer when the million or more Yanks were trained and in the field.

In any event, Dautin was now assigned to a regiment on the front lines; though his squad remained in the status of trainers. Lieutenant Monier had taken charge of the training and Dautin was glad of it. The American officers certainly responded to him more readily than they did to a mere doughboy with stripes. Monier reveled in the environment; the food and atmosphere of the officer's mess was very different from that of the French Army. He developed the habit of smoking cigarettes and constantly had one lit up now. A new routine began as Dautin and the squad instructed the companies when they rotated between the trenches in their sector every few days.

The talk in the regiment centered on the fighting in the north between the Germans and British armies at Ypres, near the Belgian border. The battle had begun in July and had already cost tens of thousands of casualties on each side. The static warfare that trench fighting had become resulted in a carnage of killing without much, if any, ground being gained by either side. In the American minds, fighting involved movement which required getting out of the trenches and onto open terrain. Many of the Yanks thought it ironic that trench warfare had really begun at the end of their own huge Civil War a half century earlier. The difference now centered on improved artillery and machine guns which made fighting in the open deadly. The ideas put forward for different tactics were not limited to any specific rank or position. Everyone voiced opinions on what should be done; this trait of the Americans amused their French mates greatly. The British seemed to think of doughboys as simply a bit backward.

"Sergeant Weldon, someone to see you." The American Captain was gesturing over his shoulder as he walked by. Looking that way, Dautin saw Earl coming toward him, trying hard not to break into a run.

"Earl. How on earth did you find me? I tried to look you up before we left Gondrecourt, but didn't get anywhere in my search."

"Well, before you left the States, I told you I'd find you if I had to search all of France; practically had to do that. It helps that I'm attached to Division; I work with communications and, since we have telephones almost everywhere, it only took a few days to track you down."

"Well, how about that. You think the job will keep you out of the fighting? That would not be a bad idea. What do you hear about the fighting up in Ypres between the Brits and the Hun?"

"Oh, it's bad and looks like it may get worse. Word at Division is that the Canadians are going in next. The New Zealand Corps has already lost nearly half their strength in three days. I hope General Pershing has better people planning things than the Limeys. They just seem to push ahead behind their artillery barrages until something bad happens, which is exactly what DOES happen."

"Anyway, what news from home? I got a bunch of letters the same day I got yours and haven't had anymore since. Mom wrote that Grandpa Isaiah was pretty sick; you know anything about that? I'd sure miss him..."

"Yeah, he's got some kind of sickness going on in his bowels. Can't seem to keep food down well and when he does, it goes all the way through real quick. He was at the doctor the day before I left home but they didn't know anything; had to wait some more to get some kind of specialist from Rochester. I haven't gotten any letters from home since I joined up; didn't even know you'd gotten mine 'til just now."

"Well, it's sure good to see you. Let's go get some chow and coffee; how long you got before you have to get back to Division? Maybe stay the night?"

"I think so; actually, I'm running wire up in this sector for a couple days. I think we can get some time together later tomorrow, too. Supper sounds great; I'm really hungry. So far Army chow's been pretty good. Course, I haven't been this close to the front lines before; think we can take a look over toward the Hun lines later?"

41

Chapter 11
October 1917

Isaiah sat in his chair, calmly looking out over the meadow. The land that sloped away from the house down to the creek held so many memories for him. He could feel the serenity it brought; the peace that flowed through him like the water from the springs in the distant woods. To a person who took the time to sit and listen, the earth seemed to speak of the years his family had already spent here. He remembered his own father, so long ago, telling of how the house would face just so, to capture the meadow like a painting to be studied and remembered. Isaiah could see his mother gazing out the window as he and his older brother carried water from the creek, or splashed in it after a hot dusty day of clearing and preparing the land for planting; the dark, nearly black color of the earth under the foot thick sod. Could it really have been so long ago? His bones recounted the years that had passed, the miles his legs had carried him. His mind argued that it wasn't so far away; the memories seemed so fresh and alive.

Isaiah Weldon was dying; the fire slowly burning down until only a few embers remained. His seventy first birthday had come and gone; bringing with it the news that his body was occupied by an enemy he felt but couldn't quite see. The doctors from Rochester agreed that he would, in all likelihood, not see another spring. The cancer that would take him to his beloved Elizabeth was too far along to stop. He had never been a quitter, had never given up without a fight. His generation had healed the country from the cancer of slavery; had built it up to become one of the greatest in the world. But this battle was on his shoulders alone and he was tired.

Just beyond the creek he could hear his dear one calling; she lay in the ground next to his own parents. His father's grave was under a granite ledge, the name carved in the stone by the hands of a kind neighbor. The same man had made a coffin from the tree which killed James Weldon as he began to clear the land.

Isaiah's mother was beside her husband and Beth, sweet Beth, was nearby; soon they would be reunited forever.

The vision dimmed as he heard the footsteps behind him. The smell of morning coffee swept past him, a fleeting memory of campfires and sleeping in tents...

"Morning, Dad. Peaceful, isn't it?"

Jack pulled over another chair and sat next to his father, handing Isaiah his favorite mug; the heat of it warmed his hand and felt right. He smiled at the thoughtful demeanor of his son and thanked his dear one for the way she had raised him.

"Good morning, Jack. I thought I'd get up a little early and enjoy the sunrise. Not too many mornings as nice as this left before the snows come; helps me relax. I have a real peaceful feeling about this whole thing. Sitting here remembering everything gives me more goodness inside than all the medicine those Mayo boys can whip up. Your mother was right when she said there are things that, uhhh, oh yeah, passes all understanding. Part of me really yearns to be with her again; mornings like this I miss her most." Soft tears slowly rolled down his cheeks.

Jack listened and was careful not to rush in with his own comments. This was a side of his father he didn't experience often. Isaiah was a man of action, of doing; it was not often the softer side of him came out. Jack could remember only a handful of times when he'd actually seen his father shed tears; the most vivid was when his mother had been buried in the woods beyond the creek. He, himself, found it easier to cry as he got older. He imagined the bond between a man and his wife was the deepest pool of feeling within; thoughts of life without his own beloved always brought a tear and that catch in his breath.

Phebe watched these two men of hers from inside the house; wishing only that Dautin could be here as well. She knew he deserved a letter about Grandpa Isaiah and his health. How to break the news to him was what had prevented her from writing. She took paper and a pen, sat down at the table and began to write.

Chapter 12
November 1917

Earl walked into the Sergeant's room of the barracks and found
Dautin sitting on the edge of his bunk holding his head. There
was a letter on the bed next to him.

"Hey, Doc; I've brought news."

"Well, I hope it's better than what I've just been reading. I got a
letter from home; Grandpa Isaiah is really sick. The doctors in
Rochester say he's got cancer and probably won't live through the
winter. You know, I just can't imagine the farm without him
offering to help and then telling one of his stories of his time in the
army. The hardest part is not being there; stuck here in this hell of
rain and mud."

Earl sat down on another bunk. "I haven't gotten any mail for a
week or longer. Guess it'll catch up with me soon. I'm sorry about
Grandpa; I know how close you two are. Even though I'm treated
just like family, I don't know, there's still something a bit different
about not being blood family. I'll sure miss that smile of his when
he winds up to spin a story. I often wonder what he'd think of the
fighting over here. I know he was in the trenches on the way to
Atlanta, but that was sure a different kind of fighting."

"He'd tell us to keep our heads down, be safe and come home.
Same thing Dad told me when I left. I'd guess he said it to you,
too, when he brought you up to Fort Snelling. Grandpa found a
way to survive the Army and we need to do the same. Dad did as
well down in Cuba and out west, against the Indians before that. I
know I learned a lot from the two of them and their stories.
Grandpa always said he remembers the best times and tries to
forget the rest. He and Will Grayson both made it through three
years of fighting and marching. I know I actually enjoy what I'm
doing; it's the waiting that's hard to take."

"Shoot, I've only been in a short time and I already find it kind of dull. Learning things through the training seemed exciting at first; it's the tenth, or the hundredth, time they tell you the same thing that gets me. You know how it is." Earl had always been quick to catch on, just like Dautin. "I suppose the time will come when things get moving so fast that a guy won't have time to think about being bored."

"I just wish we'd get into the fighting." Dautin added. "I wonder when the Generals will figure we've got enough Americans over here to finally fight. Let's get it over with, beat the Germans and go home."

"Can't answer for the top brass, but word at Division this morning is that there's been a revolution in Russia. Looks like they're going to stop fighting in the east. I suppose that means the Germans will bring all those men over here to France. Your Colonel LeBeau told you this would probably happen and looks like it is now. The Brits have stopped their attacks up at Ypres, too. I guess they figure losing half a million men in three months was enough. I don't know, Dautin; part of me hopes spring never arrives. It will bring with it fighting like no one has ever seen, I think. Half a million casualties for what? All they got was some high ground; they didn't even move the lines more than five miles."

"That's why we've got to get out of these damned trenches so we can move around when we fight. As much as I like LeBeau and the other Frenchies, I can't stand their ideas on fighting." Dautin was wrapping his puttees as he spoke. The bottoms of both legs were quickly wound snugly in the wool strips. Earl chuckled as he watched his brother get dressed.

"How long did it take you to get used to putting those on? I remember countless times having them unravel while marching. It seemed to take forever to learn just how tight to wrap them. Too loose and they'll fall off, too tight and you can't feel your feet."

"I know. You never did have the gaiters, though, did you? When I first signed up, we were issued the old leather ones; those things were terrible! Hot, stiff and when you got them soaked, they'd get so tight when they dried out, you almost couldn't stand. The canvas ones were better, but I like these. You don't even notice them once you get them right and they help keep your boots on in this damned mud. The barbed wire tears them up, though. Have

45

you noticed the cavalry wraps theirs from the top down, not like us infantry. It's one way to tell us apart, I guess."

"Yeah, that and we're not on a horse! Come on; let's find some chow and a dry place to eat it."

As they stepped out into the dim light of the new morning, Dautin mentioned how easy it would be to disappear into the mass of men on the base. All had on their helmets, overcoats and gas mask bags on their chests. Every so often a Marine, in his darker green colored uniform, would stand out. Even so, it was nearly impossible to tell one man from another; the individual soldier seemed swallowed up in the crowd.

Dautin knew he'd be transferred again soon. The training of the Marines of the Second Division, with their distinctive emblem of the Indian chief's head, was complete. They would be heading up to the front lines to take their place alongside the French for their final 'baptism of fire' before the great offensives of 1918 began. The question Doc pondered now was when his turn, and that of his squad, would come. They had been training others for months and were still anxious to be in the fighting. Another concern he had was for Earl; he hoped his brother could remain assigned to Division as part of the communications department. Dautin heard these units would be broken up and shuffled to other front line regiments when the telephone lines and other infrastructure were completed. They wouldn't even benefit from the training provided to the other soldiers but would have to learn when they were assigned to the trenches.

"Earl, have you heard anything about what's next for you? You think you'll stay at Division or be shipped to another unit? I mean, how many of you will be kept back to maintain the equipment you've been setting up?"

"I have no idea; rumors are we'll be attached to one of the army battalions in the Second Division, alongside the Marines. I suppose it could be sooner than I'd like. Aren't you almost done with their training here?"

"Actually, we finished days ago. I expect they'll be moving up to the front soon; why don't you ask your Lieutenant if you guys are going to be trained before you head out?"

"Yeah, I'll do that when I see him later today. How about you? When is your unit going to be done here?"

"Well, I expect to hear any day now whether we'll be shipped up to the front or assigned to train more of the new guys coming in. There seems to be no end to the supply of units arriving from the States. Sometimes I wish we'd just get to the fighting so we could end this thing; there must already be a million of us here."

Chapter 13
December 1917

Hospital 12

Esther walked to the door and knocked; the sign on it gave the name of the hospital administrator as Colonel James Baker, MD. She heard a simple "Enter" and opened the door, revealing a large, sunlit room with a desk at the far end. Seated behind the desk was the Colonel; a man in his mid forties with a full head of graying hair, glasses and a neatly trimmed moustache.

"Good morning, sir. I was directed to report to you on my arrival here at Mesves. My name is Esther Rundquist; I've been transferred from the French hospital near Rouen."

"Yes, Miss Rundquist. You come highly recommended; I understand you've served with the French since the start of the war? How is it you came to volunteer your services so early and here in France, at that?"

"Well, sir; I was a student in Paris in August of 1914 when the war here began. Long story short... my father must have wanted a boy; I learned how to operate automobiles back home and volunteered to drive ambulances for the French medical services. There was such a need, even a woman was accepted. I studied nursing in my off hours and have helped in the hospital since the fall of 1915... two years now. I feel it's time to help my own country with the American Expeditionary Force in France."

"Lord knows we can certainly use someone who knows their way around and speaks the language. I'd like to assign you to work with the director of our nursing staff, Mrs Williams. Most of the patients we see here at present are French themselves; as you know, the AEF is just beginning to get into the fighting. I'm sure we'll see more and more of our own men as time goes on. Meanwhile, besides your nursing duties, would you be willing to help my staff learn enough French to get by?"

"Certainly, Colonel. It will be a nice …. uh, distraction from the wards."

"Tell me, Miss Rundquist, where in the States are you from, if I may ask?"

"Wisconsin, sir; I was born in Chicago but raised along Lake Michigan outside of Racine. Most of the people in the area happened to be Norwegian and my family is Swedish. I suppose it helps me to fit in here where there have been so few Americans until recently." Esther smiled as Colonel Baker laughed and pushed away from his desk. He rose and came around to shake her hand, officially welcoming her to his hospital.

"Mrs. Williams' office is on the next floor up. The stairs are just down the hall; what say we go and introduce you to her?"

Baker opened the door and escorted Esther up to another office. "This building is for administration and supplies only. The wards are housed in the new ones you passed on your way here. The French have been busy building dozens of them for the past month. Eventually we'll have nearly 5,000 beds here and we're only one of twelve medical units at Mesves. The AEF also has more hospitals from here back to the coast; by next spring we expect to handle several thousand cases a day, so we're told. Our unit will specialize in gassing casualties; chlorine, mustard and the rest. Each of our ward buildings will be used for one of the types. I understand you have experience in gas victims, Miss Rundquist?"

"Oh, yes sir. Some of it gets quite ghastly… poor souls. I think it's the worst that can happen, really. Gas and shrapnel wounds seem to be the most debilitating and cause life long suffering."

"Anyway, there's time yet before we get any real number of casualties. I'm told it will be well into this next year before we've built up that overwhelming force we need to smash right through the Huns. One massive offensive and on to Berlin, that's what the word is."

"Pardon me for saying so, Colonel; I've heard that from the French for years, and the British. Now it's the same message from we Americans. Sometimes I really wonder if this war will ever come to an end. In the meantime, I just do the best I can and pray it'll

49

be over soon. I look forward to serving with Mrs Williams and assisting in any way I can."

At the Front

Sergeant Weldon was standing at attention in the office of Major General Bundy, commander of the Second Division. Also in the office were Dautin's squad, Colonel LeBeau and Lieutenant Monier. Colonel LeBeau was presenting members of the squad with the *Croix de guerre*, a French military decoration for heroism under fire.

"Eet ees weeth honair I geeve theese medals to you brave fighteeng men. The gratitude of France goes weeth them." LeBeau saluted each as he hung the ribbon attached to a medal around their necks. General Bundy also presented Dautin with an American award, the Bronze Star, for the courage he showed in saving the life of the French poilu during the trench raid in late July.

"Sergeant Weldon, I commend you on the successful raid you and your men accompanied the French on. I also want to extend my personal thanks to the unit for the excellent job you've all done in helping to train the Second Division. My hope is that we'll all put that fine training to good use in the coming months against the enemy. Meanwhile, I welcome you to the Division and look forward to hearing of additional good work by you. With men like you we will not accomplish less than the destruction of the German Army."

"Thank you, sir. I know I speak for all of the other men in the squad when I say we're glad to have been of service. We also are anxious to get on with the fighting, sir. Meaning no disrespect, General, but when can we get into the mix again?"

"Well, your determination is certainly admirable, Sergeant. I'll see to it you get ample opportunity to mix it up, as you say. How about showing a few of the Marines how a trench raid goes on; perhaps bring back a few Huns with you?"

"Thank you, SIR! That's what we've been wanting for some time." The other men in the squad all relaxed and smiled; Digger patted Dautin on the back and let go a laugh. Colonel LeBeau turned to General Bundy and said, "Mon General, theese man will not fail you. I knew the Sergeant's fathair in Cuba; he comes from a long line of soljairs..."

"Thank you Colonel. I'll remember that endorsement; thank you as well, Lieutenant, for the fine job you've done in helping our Division get accustomed to front line duty. Good luck and God's blessings on you both and your new commands."

With that, Dautin's connections with Colonel LeBeau and Lieutenant Monier came to an end. The French officers shared an informal time afterward with the American soldiers; in the process, several bottles of good wine and cognac were disposed of amid the somber and somewhat tearful goodbyes.

Chapter 14
January 1918

"Again? We're going over the top again tonight?" Digger had a tired and resigned expression on his face. The past two weeks had been a series of night trench raids whose purpose seemed, felt by a few in the squad, to emphasize leaving behind dead soldiers and Marines rather than in bringing back German prisoners. The numbers were not as bad as the feelings would indicate. They had gone on six missions, had brought back some twenty enemy for interrogation and had lost seven of their own; one of the original squad members and six they were training. This was a dangerous business indeed.

"Jeez, Doc, maybe we shouldn't have been so damn good at this that first time. I mean, it was great, but when Sammy bought it the other night it really hit me hard. It doesn't seem like so much of an adventure anymore; more like we're the sand in an hourglass and our time's getting closer. You know what I mean."

"Sure, Digger; I got 'ya. But we still have a job to do and if we just send these guys over without us, how many you think will make it back? One out of twelve? We've gone out seven times and lost one of our own; that leaves nine of us. I'll take those odds. Anything that gets me back to Minnesota sooner than later is alright with me."

"Yeah, OK, I'm with you. I just woke up this morning with a feeling, I don't know. I remember the old guys back home would talk about how during a war, sometimes someone would just know.... I mean KNOW... that they weren't going to make it. Maybe I should sleep facing the other way..."

Digger's premonition was on Doc's mind later as he briefed those in the squad who were going through the wire that night. They'd be taking five Marines with them; five of the squad would make the total of ten they wanted for this raid. They'd go with pistols, knives and grenades; a diversion by the artillery would attract the

Germans attention down the line about a quarter mile. They would go over at 0300 hours, three o'clock in the morning, a time when the Germans would be the most tired. Doc had decided that Digger wouldn't be going on this one; let him sit this one out.

After a couple hours of sleep, the men were awake shortly after midnight. Each made sure they were darkened; nothing shiny on their uniforms and burned cork smeared on their faces, necks and backs of the hands. Six grenades and six magazines for their pistols were handed out per man. Doc noticed that one of the Marines was really just a kid; he'd seen young ones before but this one had never even shaved. As they checked over their gear, this Marine's trench knife slipped out of his hand and fell, skewering the foot of the man next to him. Doc had the man taken to the rear by a medic; now they were down one and hadn't even left the trench. Digger came up and started to get undressed and "geared up" for the raid.

"Hell, Doc. Don't say anything; there is no way I'm not going on this with you. Haven't missed one yet and sure won't watch from back here as you get your butt blown off or something."

"Well, it is a big enough target I suppose. Listen; you take the midpoint back a bit and don't do any of your stupid stuff, you know. This one hasn't started well; let's get it over with and the drinks will be on me."

"Hey, that alone makes it worth going along!"

They waited and watched and waited a bit longer before they heard the sound of the artillery going over on its mission to distract the enemy. Quietly and with little motion, Doc slipped over the top of the trench and into the first of the shell holes out front. Watching the team, it was easy to spot the members of his squad. The new guys just weren't as familiar with this syle of movement and crawled more like they were back in training; a bit noisier and with limbs sticking up and out just that little bit more when they moved. They crossed over into the German's zone without being detected. Sliding into an enemy trench Doc and Corporal Adams, the Marine squad leader, signaled to the others to fan out and get their grenades ready.

A German sentry was a few yards ahead and, when he lit up a cigarette, Doc pounced knowing the man would be temporarily blinded by the match. He had his knife at the Hun's throat before the match even went out. Adams and Digger found the entrance to a German dugout and, pointing their pistols inside, whispered "Hande hoch" just loud enough to wake those inside. Four more of the enemy were added, along with another sentry. So far they'd not had to make any noise; it looked like things were going well.

The squad managed to get themselves and the captives out of the trench and were back in 'no man's land" when the first flare popped overhead and that brilliant, harsh white light silhouetted them. A German machine opened up from behind them, answered by one from the American side.

"Everyone down." Doc yelled this even as he slid into a crater to his left. He landed in the water and mud in the bottom, right on top of what used to be a man. Swallowing his disgust, Doc looked up at the rim of the hole to see, against the light of another flare, a Marine disappear in the blast of a mortar round as it landed. Knowing they had to keep moving, he hollered for everyone to head for their lines. Doc crawled out of the shell hole and saw the boots of the man he'd just seen blown to pieces sitting there like they were on display. He could just identify others of the squad on their way to the American lines. The last man in line was next to him as Doc came up. The two of them made sure their prisoners didn't try to go back; it wasn't that hard as everyone just wanted to get closer to the American lines to live.

As they reached the edge of the trench, and safety, one of the Germans raised his head just a few inches. It seemed to blow up as machine gun bullets ripped into it, spraying blood and brains over the men standing in the trench below. As he slid down into the waiting hands of friends, Doc glanced up and saw Digger's smile turning into a grimace. A bullet had smashed into his collar bone, breaking it and just missing his neck.

"Million dollar wound, I'd say. That should keep you from having to go out there again for awhile. Corporal, get a medic and see to him. Let's get a count on who we've got here and get the prisoners back to the command area for questioning."

"Sergeant, we're missing two Marines and one prisoner."

54

"Two? You're sure?" Doc had seen the one blown up but hadn't realized another was gone.

He went over the mission in his head and couldn't figure it; must have been while he was in the crater. Stupid, falling into it like that; have to be more careful next time. Then he chuckled to himself at the ridiculous thought; careful? This whole God awful situation he was supposed to be the expert at....

Chapter 15
February 1918

Doc and his men were sprawled over the soft green grass of the lawn behind the chateau that served as the regimental headquarters. Most were asleep; grateful for the opportunity to get an hour of "shuteye" with the sun warming them. One of the men was obviously enjoying a dream feast as he periodically let forth with deep sighs and moans of glutinous pleasure. Doc smiled and went on examining the soil his hands held. The light brown dirt was so different than that back home; he wasn't sure you could even get a good corn crop out of this soil. Too much clay he surmised, though that made for great trenches and field fortifications.

He heard footsteps approaching on the gravel pathway that led to the lawn. Looking up Doc saw the company adjutant looking at the faces of the men lying around. Doc softly said, "Over here", and the adjutant nodded, waved and headed his way.

"Sergeant Weldon, you asked to be notified if any more information came up about the missing Marine from the raid last week. I'm sorry to say his body has been recovered. He was found in a Hun trench, not far from the one you led the raid on. They found him tied hand and foot with his throat cut; it looked like he was being interrogated when he was killed. The Captain thinks he must have gotten his directions mixed up during the mortar fire and headed the wrong way, back to the German lines."

"Thanks. Sometimes guys just up and disappear; it's better when we know what happened, even if it isn't good news."

"I do have more info for you. A message was sent over for you from Division. Your brother has been reassigned to the 32nd Division's signal section to continue working on setting up their communications. He mentioned in the note to be sure to tell you, ahhh, that you're not to worry your pretty head about him anymore." The adjutant finished the message with a grin.

"Yeah, that sounds like my brother. Can you let the Captain know our squad will be heading up to the Fifth Marine's position in a few hours? As soon as the sun is down we're going to get some chow and report to them for a week or so; their turn for some raids, I suppose."

"Sure, Sergeant, I'll let him know right away. Good luck and good hunting."

Doc had just enough time to go to the battalion aid station and visit Digger before he moved up with the squad. Walking across the regimental area he was greeted by several of the men he'd trained in the past weeks since his transfer from the Division area at Gondrecourt. One in particular, a private named Nelson from eastern Wisconsin, caught his eye. Doc stopped as Nelson hurried over.

"Good afternoon, Sergeant Weldon. You probably don't remember me; name's Nelson... uhh, Stan Nelson. I've wanted to speak to you since we finished our time with you. I'm wondering if your squad has need of someone like me? I know we'll all get into the action later this spring, but I'd really like to pitch in before that. Any chance of my transferring or being assigned to your squad?"

"I don't really know, Nelson. Why don't you talk to your company officers and they can go through the necessary channels. I do know the squad is a couple of men short of what we had when we began the training cycles. What I've never actually looked into is replacing them. Now that you mention it; it wouldn't be a bad idea to have a few more in the bunch. We've come through the past weeks with two or three gone. I'm heading to the aid station right now to visit one of the guys; he got hit in the shoulder last week. I need to see when he'll be coming back."

"Thanks, Sarge. I'll check with my 'Louie' and see what he says. Thanks a lot, really."

The more Doc thought about it, the more he liked the thought of getting a few replacements. There seemed to be enough soldiers at hand; maybe he could even arrange for a couple of Marines to join the team. It was certainly worth looking into the next time he spoke with Captain Lewis, his own company commander.

Chapter 16
March 1918

Doc felt he knew the contents of the letter before he opened it; the news in the last one from home told of the decline of Grandpa's health. As he sliced the enveloped open, he said a silent prayer for Isaiah and his parents. He sat on a grassy patch, the only one around and began to read.

"March 3rd
Oakview Minn
Dear son,
I'm writing this to you a few hours after we laid Grandpa to rest next to Gramma Beth in the woods across the creek. I know he wouldn't want us to trouble you in any way right now; he'd say you've enough on your mind "keepin' your head from being blown off". Mother and I have had our time to grieve even before the end came yesterday. Your grandfather led a life full of love and adventure; that is, in a way, what every man wants. Now he's again with the love of his life, this time forever.

We pray that this letter finds you in good health and in a place where you can take a few minutes to reflect on the man my father was and the place he had in your own life. If you can take time to visit Earl, I would appreciate it. I know, from his last letter, there are many miles between you right now. It would be good for both of you to see each other."

The letter continued with more comments on events around the farm. His dad always wrote of the weather, what friends he'd run into; just the sort of things they would talk about sitting together on the porch back home. Doc so appreciated the letters from his family; he read them again and again until they were well worn. When he received a new one, he carefully placed the last in a growing pile, tied tightly with a bootlace and wrapped the bundle in a piece of rubberized canvas to keep them dry.

He was distracted by the sound of an airplane above him. You never could tell when one would suddenly swoop down to machine gun the troops on the ground. This time, Doc had a front row seat for the first real dogfight he'd seen. As he watched, several more planes appeared from different directions and began a noisy sort of dance, like bees buzzing in a field. The faint pup-pup-pup of the machine guns firing at each other was often hard to hear with the sounds of the engines straining in a climb or whining loudly in a dive. Doc was held, transfixed, by what he was watching. All of a sudden, one plane began to trail smoke and he could just see the fire engulf the front of the plane. It started to twirl down and around, spiraling toward the earth. He watched as the whole plane seemed to be burning. He saw the pilot jump out of the craft and plummet to the ground, followed by the fiery wreck of what had been his plane. Two more planes, one painted a bright yellow, also began to burn and fall from the sky. He noticed a group of a dozen or so other soldiers straining to see every detail above them.

The air show was over in minutes; Doc had seen seven aircraft destroyed in that short time. Several others had flown off trailing smoke, engines sputtering as they limped home. Just like that, he thought, seven men died. He could not even imagine the horror it must be to know you have to make the choice; burn alive or fall to your death by jumping. He had seen men going up in the big gas-filled balloons that were used for artillery spotting and knew they wore parachutes in case they were attacked. However, he couldn't understand why pilots didn't wear them as well; convinced that he certainly would. Then he reminded himself that he'd never fly in one of those confounded things anyway.

A few days later Doc was on his way to see Earl; he'd obtained a three day pass from his company commander. It seems Captain Lewis had lost a brother a few weeks earlier in a train wreck in Arizona and could understand Doc's request. He hitched a ride with a truck transporting supplies to the same town Earl's signal unit was assigned to; it took nearly the entire day to get there through the snarled traffic behind the American lines and the myriad of small French towns along the way. As the truck passed one group on the roadside, Doc noticed the drooped shoulders and downcast looks on all of the civilians; saw the rough carved, wooden shoes they wore. For them the war had been going on for nearly four years and supplies of everything had nearly run out. Even the leather for belts and shoes now went to the Army. He also noticed that all he saw were old men, women and little children. The price of this war in the lives of the young men was a high one for France. The cheering people he'd seen when he arrived nine long months before had faded back into the reality of a nation at war. With Russia out of the fight everyone was getting ready for the waves of German soldiers they knew would attack soon. The Boche had to win the war before the Americans could organize the millions that were, even now, pouring across the sea.

Doc imagined that most of Europe resembled the area he'd been through. He wondered about the doughboys he'd met, and trained, that still spoke the languages of Europe. There were also many whose parents had immigrated to the States from the continent in the years before the war. He imagined that there were soldiers in the American army who could trace family back, just a generation or so, to this area of France. Perhaps they were alive today simply because someone, a few years earlier, had decided to leave on a chance for a new and better life in the land of promise.

The truck stopped; the driver told Doc this was as close as they would be to Earl's unit. He hopped out of the truck and thanked the man. It was then he realized that during the entire ride, he'd not heard a single word of English from any of the half dozen others on the truck. He knew two of them had been conversing in Norwegian or Swedish, he really couldn't tell which. Two others had been talking to each other in what sounded like Spanish; he remembered some of the guys at Fort Snelling that would practice speaking it in case they went down to Mexico. Doc chuckled to himself as he began to walk to find Earl; what he'd imagined when he saw those poor civilians was true. How odd that so many of the new doughboys arriving now didn't even speak the language of the country they were fighting for. Most of those who enlisted right away a year before were 'regular' Americans, or what he had considered that to be. Now units showed up speaking a dozen or more languages and often had to be told several times what was required of them. He couldn't wait to tell his father what this was like; it was surely an American army on the move.

He found Earl's outfit and was told to wait awhile; Earl was out setting up telephone equipment in a command location a few miles away. Doc found out where it was located and decided to 'hoof it' over there to find his brother. After about a mile's walk, he spotted a Corporal, two new stripes bright on his tunic, carrying a coil of wire and other equipment; maybe he'd know where Earl was. The smile on the man's face as he turned at the sound of Doc's voice told him he'd found more than the information he was looking for. Earl threw down the stuff he'd been carrying and gave Doc a good old Minnesota bear hug. The two spent the time walking back reminiscing about Grandpa Isaiah, retelling each other so many of the stories they'd been told growing up. No tears, just good laughs and fond memories. They promised each other to put their own medals, whatever they came home with, on his grave in the woods; to honor the man for his own fight to save the country so long ago.

The two shared a bottle of wine they bought on the way through the village Earl was billeted in. His room was shared by four men in a house owned by one of the few civilians who hadn't moved out earlier. Her name was Madame LeFleur and she was pleased to cook for the eight men that lived in her home. One more mouth didn't seem to matter at all. Doc feasted on roasted chicken and a fresh garden salad. He had eaten little homemade food since getting to France and relished every mouthful. The other men in Earl's unit hooted and howled as Doc packed away the food. Their war, so far, had been very different from his in the front lines. After dinner and the wine Doc was almost asleep on his feet as he told Earl's buddies of what trench life was like.

"I'm not saying it's the worst place to be, but it's darned close. Not at all like the practice trenches we all played in back in the States. The smell, well you just about get used to it, stop gagging, you know, when all of a sudden another *whiz-bang* or *ash can* comes over from the Huns and 'WHAM', it digs up more bodies the last shelling just covered. When you're up front, you've got these shovels piled up every few yards, to dig guys out when a shell buries them. You've got to be quick or they'll suffocate under the dirt. After a few days, you learn how to sleep during the day and work at night when no one sees each other. It sure isn't all glory and honor like we thought when we signed on..... it's more like gore and horror."

Most of the guys were silent when he'd finished, their mouths hung open. They had only been in France a couple of months themselves, but had not yet rotated up to the front. None of them had seen the bodies or smelled that mixture of burnt cordite, dead bodies and stale mustard gas. Their own experiences, so far, had been soft beds and good hot food. They all knew their own time was coming. One young kid, barely old enough to shave, spoke up.

"Sergeant, it can't be that bad all the time, can it. What about when you get relieved, so you can, ahhh, relieve yourself?"

"Son, relieving yourself is the other reason for those shovels I spoke of. You take one, put a little dirt on the blade and, well, add your own. Then you sort of fling it out of the trench. Hopefully, the shell hole you throw it into doesn't have anybody in it, you know.... a target."

Earl looked at Doc and broke up, laughing. "You sound just like Grandpa Isaiah now; you even look like him when you say those things. Oh, Lord, one's gone and another's just arrived."

The next morning Doc was able to hitch another ride with a light artillery unit heading to the front near his regiment. As the trucks wound their way through the town his squad was billeted in when they rotated back from the trenches, Doc noticed two changes that had taken place in the past couple of weeks. The first was the pile of rubble that was once the barn he and his men slept in; the apparent target of a recent aerial bombing. The second change was much more pleasant. A new building was nearby, the fresh lumber walls not yet painted. Workmen were raising a sign above the front façade; it announced 'Red Cross – YMCA'. He had heard of the nice folks there and the donuts, coffee and hospitality offered by them. Doc looked forward to his own rotation from the front next week; he'd have a chance to visit and get some good coffee. First he'd have to find a new place for his men to sleep.

Chapter 17
April 1918

Doc could sense the presence of the enemy soldiers; it was too dark to see them and they weren't making a sound. The hair on his neck bristled like when you know someone's talking about you. He slid, quietly, into the shell hole next to him and crawled over the pieces of several bodies. The thought that they might actually all have belonged to one man went through his mind and then vanished. "Focus, don't let that crap crowd out the important..."

Doc crawled up the side of the crater, careful not to let his helmet betray him by getting too far above the rim. He could see the glow of the German's pipe, caught a whiff of the acrid smoke from his *ersatz* tobacco. A bead of sweat ran down Doc's nose, threatening to make him sneeze when it tickled his upper lip. He slowly raised his pistol up, knowing he'd have to make two quick shots and both had better damn well count. The multiple sounds of the gun mingled into one loud noise; with cat-like speed and agility, Doc was up and out of his hole and into the Germans'. One of the men he'd shot was still alive and moving; at least until Doc dispatched him with a quick thrust of his trench knife. He wriggled up to the rim of his newly acquired gun pit and signaled for the rest of the squad to move up. There were still several yards to go until they entered the enemy trench itself. Two others slipped in beside Doc before the machine gun opened up on them. A third man, just sliding over the rim, was nearly cut in two by the spray of bullets; dead before he hit the bottom. At that moment a German grenade, looking like one of his mother's potato mashers, tumbled in the middle of them. One man yelled and tried to climb out; Doc threw his own body on top of it without a moment's hesitation. It didn't go off; the man throwing it had forgotten to pull the priming cord. Doc got up off the grenade, his heart almost busting out of his chest.

"I'm feeling too old for this; I think my hair will gray by the time I'm twenty five." he whispered.

"Hell, Doc; you move like a damn bullet yourself. I hardly even saw that thing before you were on it. You'da been blown to kingdom come for sure if the Heinie had known what he was doing when he threw it."

Doc took a few deep breaths to calm himself and looked down at the dead doughboy at his feet. He rolled him over and recognized Nelson, the kid that was so eager to join the squad a few short weeks ago. Now he was mad; it was bad enough they tried to blow him up. He swallowed hard and put the image of Nelson's begging him to transfer out of his mind. He could think more on that when he wrote the kid's folks a letter tomorrow; better to shut off that part of his thinking right now.

"Come on. We've got work to do before we can relax anymore. When we hit the Hun trench, you go right. I'll head left; toss two grenades ahead of yourself, maybe twenty feet. Be sure to look down when they go off or you'll not see anything, maybe forever..."

The two of them crawled up and out of the hole and found the wire in front of the enemy position blown apart. They made it into the trench ahead as the others in the squad followed. Their four grenades punctured the quiet; then it seemed like all hell broke loose. At least three machine guns opened up, spraying the air just above their heads; the bullets making that peculiar metallic zinging through the air. Doc saw a German officer try to slip up the backside of the trench; his head came clean off as he raised it above the ground. Doc slipped past the still twitching body, tossing a grenade in the opening of a dugout as he went by. The blast was followed by anguished cries and groaning. The man behind him threw another in and there was only silence after the second explosion.

Twenty minutes later, which seemed like as many hours, the squad was back inside the American lines again. Doc lit up a cigarette and dropped into a corner. The others were also lighting up or accepting drinks offered; the prisoners they'd collected were already being herded back for interrogation and confinement. Sutton was busy telling everyone about Doc and how he'd thrown himself on that grenade; already the story was he'd saved three guys, not just the two of them. Doc knew by morning he'd hear it was the whole damn regiment!

The next day they rotated back to the village for another break; two weeks of rest, refitting with new equipment and uniforms. A chance to gain relief from the Huns and the cooties, the two real enemies of this war, was always welcome. The squad was billeted in a storeroom above a shop down the street from the new Red Cross building. Doc and the others knew it would not be as quiet as the old barn had been, but the cots were comfortable and the donuts, coffee and free cigarettes were only a couple hundred yards away. He, for one, was content that first day to wash off the mud from the front lines and get his new uniform ready. He carefully pulled the stitches from his Sergeant's chevrons to sew them on his new tunic. When that was done, he made sure to take all the other brass insignia off the collar and place them correctly on as well. Having done what the army considered a priority, Doc stretched out on a cot and fell asleep.

Getting used to sleeping through the night and being awake during the day always took a bit of time; life in the trenches was so opposite of normal. The second, or maybe it was the third, day of their stay in town Doc and Digger were reunited. They met up at the Red Cross, Doc having his second donut and third cup of coffee of the morning. Digger came up, looking a little pale and about 20 pounds heavier than he'd been the night he was wounded. The smile on his face told Doc that his friend was healed and ready to get back to work.

"About the only two things I'll miss now are the better food and the much better looking faces I'll have to stare at. Those nurses sure were prettier than a bunch of dog faced doughboys."

"Yeah, yeah... did I miss something? Were you gone for awhile? I hadn't even noticed that you weren't around. Wait... it did seem awfully quiet these past weeks."

"You sure know how to make a fella welcome, Sergeant Weldon. I guess my luck is still good; I get back to find you guys rotated from the front. Guess I'll get a few more days of rest before getting back into action."

"Well, I suppose I'll have to find some way to trim you back down to the right size. Your butt looks like it grew too big to get under the wire, you know. Can't have something that size waving in the wind for the Heinies to shoot at." Doc was glad Digger had returned; he'd missed him like he would his own right arm.

"Excuse me, Sergeant, would you like some writing paper and envelopes? When was the last time you sent a letter home?" The Red Cross worker was smiling as she offered a packet of paper and pencil to him. Dressed in a long khaki skirt and jacket, white blouse with a black necktie and hair done up under a black hat, she had a kind of military look about her. Doc was taken aback by her presence. Up to this time, he'd only seen the local French women, the working class farmers and town folks dressed in their usual black, expressions matching their clothing.

"Why, why... yes, thank you ma'am. I suppose I'd best write home; now while I've got the time. Thanks, thanks a lot." Doc was about three shades of red as he stammered his reply. The woman smiled again and walked away to the next bunch of soldiers.

Digger laughed. "Well, you certainly have a way with a lady. I know.... she's the first you've seen since you got here. Been almost a year and no American women to look at. I heard all those things in the hospital, even said them myself. You'll get used to it, I suppose. There are lots of our girls over here now; nurses, telephone operators, drivers, the works. Never thought the Army would find room on ships for them, though."

In a discussion with some of the other soldiers in the YMCA and Red Cross facility Doc learned that the destroyed barn was not exactly the result of a bombing attack. Apparently a German bomber, on its way to somewhere else, had been shot down and crashed into the barn. The resulting explosion had destroyed the building and killed seven doughboys who were billeted there. Doc shivered when he heard this, knowing it could easily have been his squad in there, had it happened another day.

That evening Doc and the rest of his squad gathered in the upstairs rooms they shared to toast the end of the first year of American involvement in the war with a hope that one more year would find them back at home and enjoying peace. They remembered each member of the unit that was no longer with them. Everyone was aware that a buildup of German troops had finally resulted in a new spring offensive to the north, along the British sector of the front. How soon it would work its way down to them was unknown; that it would was fairly certain. The last bottle of the local wine they purchased for their evening together was opened and shared by a more quiet and reflective group.

The pounding on the door and sounds of activity outside the windows were enough to wake them, hung over as they were. In a few minutes every man in the squad was a part of the scramble to rejoin regiments as word was passed of the German breakthrough to the north. As Doc and Digger moved along the road back to their own battalion, they shared the same thought. No more night raids and training and practice; this was the time for the American Army to finally get into the war.

Chapter 18
May 1918

<u>At the Front</u>

The Americans had been holding this sector for just over a week now, waiting for the German advance to begin. They were near the town of Catigny, halfway between Amiens and Rheims, about 70 miles north of Paris. Farther to the north the British had been able to blunt the initial advances by the Kaiser's armies that started in late March. Casualties on both sides had exceeded 100,000 before the lack of supplies caused the Germans to halt. Two weeks later a new offensive had begun against the French zone, just to the south of where the Americans had been moved. Again, a stubborn defense by Allied troops had prevented, barely, a German breakthrough and drive to Paris. The Germans got close enough to bring up some huge artillery guns that were able to fire shells the 21 miles or so into the city, spreading panic and causing many Parisians to flee to towns along the English Channel in the west. These attacks by the Germans were planned by Field Marshal Hindenburg and General Ludendorff, leaders of the Kaiser's Army, to make use of troops freed up by the capitulation of Russia the previous winter. They believed Germany's best hope was a negotiated peace before the overwhelming numbers of Americans arrived in France in the coming months. With a Major breakthrough and threat to the French capital, Germany could begin those negotiations from a position of strength.

It was now critical that American General Pershing and his mostly untested soldiers stand firm in the face of the veteran Germans. Orders were given to prepare defenses in depth, a tactic that would help to lessen the destructive impact of artillery bombardments on the front lines. The plan was to rush back up to the trenches when the artillery fire ceased just prior to the German advance. The few men who were to remain in the outposts ahead of the main trench lines knew the danger they had to face; if the reinforcing troops didn't come up in time, they would have to hold the line until they were killed. Doc's unit was posted about fifty yards from a canal that the Germans would have to cross in the first minutes of their attack. The Americans were supported by six heavy machine guns that had been dug in with intersecting fields of fire, creating a two hundred yard wide killing zone that extended to the far side of the canal. Doc, Digger and the rest of the squad were spread out, spaced nearly five yards apart for the length of the trenches. Boxes of grenades were within reach of each man, along with his 1903 Springfield and several hundred rounds of ammunition. Each of the heavy machine guns had four men assigned; one from each gun had been put into a mobile reserve to quickly stop any breakthrough by the Germans. A Lieutenant, in charge of the machine gun detachment, was in overall command.

The morning of the attack began with thick fog along the canal. The German preparation for crossing it could be heard but not seen. Orders were quietly passed down the line to refrain from the temptation to fire blindly toward the sounds. At the same time daylight began to filter through the fog, the enemy barrage began. The sounds of their guns firing from a mile or more to the east was quickly followed by enormous explosions just behind the squad's forward position, effectively cutting them off and isolating them. Now Doc realized the wisdom in digging the new outposts so far in front of the original trenches. The Germans must think all the Americans were still in the positions farther back.

"Alright, boys, this is it. They'll be coming soon. The fog is just lifting off the ground; we'll be able to see them and they can't call in artillery fire on top of us for some time, at least until the fog's gone. Let's make them pay for each step on this side of the canal." Doc shouted this out, knowing his words would be passed down to both ends of the line.

"Let's hope a runner makes it to us when we're supposed to pull out and head back to the trenches." said Digger. Doc nodded at him, a grim look on his face.

"Oh, Jeez, I forgot. Well, I don't feel much like retreating today anyway. Listen, Doc; I've got a letter in my pocket here..."

"Shut your mouth, Digger. You're going to deliver that letter yourself, or tear it up if you'd like. Let's just do what we know how to do. Stick to the plan and hope the rest of the regiment does, too."

The fog lifted another foot and Doc could just see the near edge of the canal. Nobody had crossed yet, but he could see waves lapping the shore, like those from the front of a boat approaching. He signaled to the nearest machine gun position and pointed. The gun began to fire with its own 'put-put-put' sound and immediately the screams and shouts from out on the water could be heard.

"Open fire, they're just beyond the water's edge."

The fog was dissipating quickly now from the sun's rising and the wind from the artillery explosions behind them. Doc could clearly see the enemy as they waded to shore, led by the hated *Stosstruppen*, the elite German soldiers specially trained, as Doc's own unit was, in trench warfare. They were approaching with *flamenwerfers* in the lead, each loaded down with a large round pressure tank of flammable liquid that squirted flames which stuck and burned everything it came in contact with. Doc's men began concentrating their fire on these men, trying to hit the tanks to make them explode. When one did, it engulfed the man carrying it, and several others nearby, with a roar and a huge ball of fire.

A man to Doc's left shouted that a machine gun was being set up to his front. Doc, Digger and another man quickly threw two grenades apiece in that direction. When the smoke from the explosions cleared, several bodies and the parts of the machine gun were scattered around. Doc watched as the soldier who had alerted them to it grinned, turned to fire again and disappeared in the explosion of a German trench mortar round. One of the reserve men ran, ducking down, to take his place.

An instant later, American and French artillery rounds began to land out along the edge of the canal, creating an impenetrable wall of smoke, fire and debris. Dozens of these big shells landed among the Germans as they were attempting to cross the water. Doc was amazed anyone could live through something so horrible; but amazed or not, he had to keep shooting at those who continued to show up on this side of the canal. The fighting continued for more than a half hour before the Germans gave up the attempt.

When the rest of their regiment arrived to relieve them, Doc and Digger took a few moments to survey the area. It was not safe, or smart, to venture towards the water. From where they stood though they could see a carpet of dead and wounded Germans, piled two or three deep along the very edge of the water. Their own losses were quite light; out of the forty in his squad and the two dozen machine gunners, they had lost less than twenty, including the Lieutenant. Doc felt bad that he hadn't gotten to know the man; he only knew his name was Reynolds. The officer had never even mentioned where he was from. Captain Lewis came up to the two as they stood staring at the dead Germans.

"Quite a view, huh?"

"Yes, sir. Pretty well calmed down now, though. A bit ago it was much more, uhh, dramatic."

"Well, according to Division, this was a feint; meant to distract us from the larger attack down on the right about mile. You can still hear that one; it's not over yet. In fact, we may be moving there shortly. Third battalion is to take our place here if we go. It looks as if the Germans are going to learn a thing or two about we Americans before today is over. One of the good things is that we get to fight on the defensive before having to 'go over the top' at them first. We all need to see what a mess it is to blindly attack prepared positions, right Sergeant?"

"Well, sir; I suppose I won't always be getting at them in the dark. I'd much rather go in from the side you know, flanking them, than right up the middle. The way our machine guns tore into them; I'd hate to be on the receiving end of anything like that."

"Hmmm, more than likely that will come, too, one day. When we go at the Huns, and we're sure to do it before too long now, they'll be in the trenches with the prepared positions, machine guns and all the rest. We'd best be thinking of a way to outfox them. In the meantime, you take what's left of your squad back and replenish your ammunition. Let your Lieutenant know when you're ready."

"Will do, sir. Any chance of grabbing some hot chow while we're back there, Captain? My men haven't eaten since last evening. I've got some guys that get much hungrier than I do."

"I'm sure your man Digger, here, could round up something to eat?"

"Why, Captain, sir; I had no idea you knew anything about me." Digger said, with a surprised smile.

"Well, Corporal, just because I don't always let things be known, doesn't mean I don't know them."

"Captain, with due respect; as soon as I figure out what you just said, I'll know how to feel about it."

Hospital 12

The hospital wards were filling fast; Esther and the other administration personnel were doing what they could to assist the nursing staff. Additional beds had been bought, and borrowed, from every source available. Even stretchers and simple tick mattresses were arranged in rows on the floor, filled with wounded doughboys and soldiers of other nations. Esther's day had already been a full one; directing the unloading of supplies and the wounded as well as assisting in the prioritizing of treatment of the wounded. The French had recently started this practice called triage. Now a nurse came up with a new problem, one Esther hadn't heard of before. There was an American Sergeant from Alabama who was not content to share a ward with wounded Negro soldiers; apparently he was creating quite a fuss about it. Esther spoke with the man; he was part of the First Division, assigned next to a French Moroccan brigade when he was wounded.

"Let me understand, Sergeant. You've fought alongside black soldiers for weeks and will not be satisfied sleeping in the same room as black Americans?"

"Yes, ma'am. My people have never consented to sleep with those people. I demand a new location; 'course you could always move them out instead."

"Well, soldier, you're in luck." The younger nurse looked at Esther with a surprised expression, mouth practically hanging open. "You see, we've just opened a new ward; one with plenty of fresh air and running water. How'd you like to be moved into it?" She was speaking so nicely, with such a sweet smile on her face that the soldier quickly assented.

"Why yes, ma'am. That'd be just right; fresh air, running water. I'd like that a heap."

"Fine. Nurse Connor here will see that you're moved right away. I'll just be a minute explaining it to her."

"Thank you, ma'am. There's just no way I'd want to be in this h'yar room with a bunch of them types; you know what I mean?"

Esther took Nurse Connor by the elbow and led her a few yards away, out of earshot of the Sergeant. She smiled at the confused nurse who, she could see, was beginning to get a bit angry. "Take the fine Sergeant to the new ward." Esther began quite loudly, glancing around to be sure he was trying to hear every word. The Sergeant had a wide smile on his face. Esther lowered her voice; "Take his bed and have four orderlies move it, carry it, out into the grassy area on the far side of the building. When you leave him, be sure to mention that the running water will begin shortly; I believe it's supposed to begin raining soon."

"Yes, Mrs Rundquist. I understand, ma'am." The nurse could hardly contain her giggles as she left to get the orderlies. Esther returned to the soldier.

"I see, Sergeant, that your wound is not too severe. I think a 'minor contusion', especially one that doesn't incapacitate, warrants no more than a day or so here. By the way, just how did you arrange to be admitted? I'd say your case seems rather trifle."

"Well, I don't want to brag none, but our regimental doctor is my uncle. When he saw me at the aid station, he said he owed it to his sister to look after me."

"I see. Well, Sergeant, be assured we, too, will look after you. Nurse Connor will be right back with four nice, strapping orderlies to take care of you."

An hour later Esther sent two orderlies outside to retrieve the bed, so recently vacated by a Sergeant she was certain was well on his way back to his regiment and his uncle. She hoped she'd have the opportunity to hear more about his case from his doctor.

As Esther was making her way back to her station in the administrative hall she happened to pass through the ward that had been the scene with the Sergeant. She was surprised, and a bit thrilled, by the round of applause and cheering she received from the other patients. She smiled in acknowledgement and some of the fatigue she had been feeling was gone; her step was much livelier the remainder of her shift.

Oakview

The rural mail carrier drove his vehicle up to the barn. James heard the sound of it and came out, wiping his hands clean from the grease he'd been putting on a wagon axle. He saw the steam coming from under the hood of the Model T; the carrier was already cussing.

"Really, you'd think I'da known better. Buying one of these danged contraptions and hoping it'd work better than the horse did. Only had to feed, water and groom the horse; seems like I'm forever changing tires and working on this blasted thing."

"Morning, Roscoe. Seems like you could use something to cool you off as well as your truck, eh? If you've got any mail for us, why don't you go bring it in to Phebe and Sam and I'll take a look at the Ford; see what we can do."

"Why thanks, Mr Weldon. That's kind of you; I do happen to have a couple of letters for you. One's from Dautin and the other's from some..., let's see, a Colonel Stratton or someone, kinda hard to read. I'll bring 'em in to Mrs Weldon."

"Hey, Sam; come out here and give me a hand with this, will'ya? Better bring that jack and the axle wrench, too."

About fifteen minutes later, the carrier returned; he had with him something wrapped in a towel and a much more pleasant demeanor. Jack knew if anyone could settle down an irate public servant, it was his Phebe.

"That missus of your's, Mr Weldon. You'd be best to never let her go."

74

"Don't plan to, Roscoe. Did she have something cool for you to drink, I hope?"

"Yes, sir. Seems you've got about the best tastin', coolest well water in these parts. She was so 'bliged about me bringing up the mail, she practically forced a piece of apple pie on me, too. Said she had too many dried apples so she made two pies up just this morning."

"That's what I've been smelling all morning. Oh, boy! I can't wait for lunch." Sam was just crawling out from under the Model T. Jack had found the leak and repaired the hose, along with putting a patch on a punctured tire he'd found in Roscoe's back seat.

"Well, Roscoe; you might think about getting a water pump for this girl. Ford used to have them on the engines and then went to a different system a few years ago. I think a pump is less sensitive to your kind of driving, with the mail route and all. You're fine to finish the day; at least the car is. That chunk of pie might put you to sleep if you eat it all at one sitting. You might want to save some until you get home."

"Naaah, then I'd have to divvy it up with my son. He's home for a few days before he ships over to France himself. Seems like a boy hardly turns eighteen afore he gets snapped up by the Army these days. I heard there's been some frightful fightin' over there with the Huns running over the Brits and all."

"Well, it could be the last desperate gamble on their part to end this thing before we get all our boys over there. Once we do, there'll be no stopping us. At least that's what I think."

"You'd know best, Mr Weldon. I still 'member when you came back from Cuba. Your pa, God bless him, was about the proudest peacock in Oakview. All of us were glad you made it back; now you're along with us hopin' all our boys come home, too."

"I sure am, Roscoe. Dautin's been in the fighting from the start and Earl's nearly finished with his special assignment; I'm sure he will be moved up to the front soon, if he hasn't already. Well, you'd best be delivering the mail; I'm going to go have what's left of that pie and read a couple of letters."

Jack and Sam walked over to the pump and washed up before they went into the house. Phebe was sitting at the kitchen table reading Dautin's letter. Jack gave her a kiss on the forehead and picked up the letter from Colonel Stratton:

Jack,
I'm sorry I can't say much, what with censorship and all. Not assigned to a command, doing administration instead. Things here are very busy, you can guess why by reading the papers, I'm sure.

I have sad news to pass along. LeBeau, our good friend, was killed a few days ago north of here during the German's latest push. You'll appreciate, I'm sure, that he died at the head of his regiment as they defended a very important transportation junction. Just his luck, I suppose; to go out as a hero of France, instead of quietly like you and I will. I had the chance to see him a week or so before the latest campaign began. He was glad for the opportunity to command again; was tired of riding herd over foreigners like you and I did with him in Cuba. I told him we understood that better than most. I wanted to tell you instead of you chancing upon an article in some local paper or what not.

I'll be sure to look up your boys when I get a chance; sorry things have not allowed me the time to do so since I got here.

Your friend, Tom

Jack put down the letter and turned to Phebe, tears in his eyes. She reached out and took his hands in hers, glancing at the letter on the table, seeing LeBeau's name and guessing at its contents.

"He was such a man of emotions; like the one I married."

"Strange. I can still see him standing tall, laughing at the rest of us hugging the dirt as the Spaniards' bullets zipped over our heads. I'm sure he died with that smile of his taunting the enemy. Glad we had the chance to see each other again. He'd tell me right now there's no need for tears. He's with his son and that means everything to him. I'll write a letter to his wife; never did meet her but I'm sure he mentioned me at least once. Tom will be able to get it to her, I hope."

Chapter 19
June 1918

<u>At the Front</u>

They took the damn town and held it; after a year of training and practice, of being told by their French allies they were not yet ready. When they went over the top days earlier they knew the whole world was watching and waiting to see just how these Americans would perform. The First Division showed that Uncle Sam had sent his boys to fight, and die, alongside the other nations allied against the Kaiser and his hordes.

With the help of French flamethrowers, the *poilus* carrying tanks of liquid hell, and a handful of the new tanks, the doughboys had advanced into the town on top of the hill. Doc was told the story of a stone mason who was found to help; he had lived and worked in the town before the Germans came. The man who had spent most of his life building and repairing the houses and shops in the town drew maps and described each of the stone structures that the enemy had now turned into a series of nearly impregnable positions interlocked with machine guns. Each basement had been converted into bunkers that shielded German soldiers with thick walls of stone and the heavy timber flooring of the houses provided cover from anything but a direct hit by artillery.

They had gone in early; the dim light and morning fog their best protection from the machine guns. Doc thought, at the beginning of the advance, that nothing could stand against the determination of those men alongside him in the trench. When the initial artillery barrage was beginning to move ahead at its "twenty five yard per minute" pace and the tanks began to rumble out on the flanks, he had seen the look in a poilu's eyes. The man, carrying one of the heavy flamethrowers, had a look of focused hatred; not for the town ahead, nor the buildings it was made of. The look was directed at the men inside the houses, the cancer of occupation they were to him, to his nation. He was the tool that would burn out the infection and restore the health of France.

77

Whistles blew, men climbed up the ladders and began the assault; following the tanks through the wire ahead. As they reached the first small building on the outskirts of the village, Doc was up front, a bit ahead of the first line. He pitched a grenade through an opening, a firing slit cut into the basement wall. The explosion was muffled by the thickness of the stone; wisps of smoke curled out the slit as a dozen or more Germans emerged from the side of the house. With their hands reaching upward they stumbled into the early gray of dawn with their shouts of *'kamerad, kamerad'* echoing in the morning air. Doc and Digger covered them with their rifles, motioning the bunch to head back toward the American lines. A moment later Doc turned at the roaring sound, felt a faint heat from behind. Turning, he saw the poilu, a wicked smile on his face as the man loosed his liquid death on the prisoners. Men screamed, running frantically around like living firebrands, bumping into each other until the flames had consumed each of them. The French soldier looked Doc in the eyes, his image wavered through the heated air between them.

"Maintenant ils sont prêts à entrer l'enfer.", the poilu shouted, pointing to the next house ahead. Doc nodded in agreement that the Huns were now ready to enter Hell.

"Holy mother of God! Brother, remind me to stay on his good side," Digger quipped as he reloaded his Springfield. Doc grabbed another grenade from the bag hanging over his shoulder and motioned up the street. One of the large Schneider tanks blew up ahead from a direct hit by a German artillery round. As they watched, hearing the screams of the crew inside, flames shot out through the ventilation slits in the side; exploding ammunition in the tank peeled part of the roof back, sending flames up into the sky. Doc skirted around a corner of the next house to find a German officer emerging from a basement entrance. Leveling his rifle at the man, Doc shouted, *"Hande hoch"*. The officer calmly reached for his pistol, his dark eyes telling Doc this was no time for surrender. The Springfield barked once and the German collapsed with a hole in the middle of his chest. Doc swore at the dead man; could not disguise his anger at the man's refusal to quit. Digger moved ahead of Doc just as a Maxim began firing from a nearby window, the bullets slicing into a man behind them. A searing stream of flame shot past Doc; he could feel its heat burning the hair on his neck. Screams and the popping of machine gun bullets going off in the fire hurried the doughboys along. This time they were both a bit more appreciative of the poilu with the flamethrower.

It took less than twenty minutes to capture the town. Doc overheard a couple of soldiers comment on how easy it would be to walk to Berlin. He and Digger shook their heads as they walked by. Their orders were to advance two hundred yards beyond the town and dig in, preparing for the counterattacks that the Germans were sure to launch. The town was not a large one but was important far beyond its size. The enemy, too, had been watching and waiting for the Americans to attack somewhere along the front. They knew they had to show the world that it made little difference; no one could stand up to the Kaiser's armies.

An hour after they finished digging their individual funk holes, the start of a new trench line, the enemy artillery began firing on the position. Shells of various sizes were falling all around them, blasting the earth into the familiar pattern of craters and torn trees. Men were tossed around like rag dolls, ripped into pieces again and again until there was no trace they had ever existed; the little that remained finally buried under the crushing dirt that seemed to fall from the very sky above them. One man jumped up, his screams going unheard in the cacophony of sound. He ran about 20 yards before disappearing in an explosion. Digger pointed to a helmet sailing through the air high above their heads.

Along with the high explosives the Germans were sending in dozens of artillery shells containing mustard gas. They would detonate with a muffled sound followed by a cloud of yellowish smoke. Heavier than the surrounding air the cloud would slowly settle toward the ground, filling shell craters and other depressions, like foxholes, with a yellow tinted fog. It burned when it came in contact with skin and would seep into food containers as well. Several men spent the first night vomiting up their tainted rations. Doc and Digger chose to go hungry rather than risk being sick; had the Germans decided that night to counter attack, the doughboys would have been easily overrun.

For two more days Doc and his squad were stuck in the partially dug forward trench; they dared not move during daylight for fear the enemy airplanes would detect the movement. If they were discovered, it was a guarantee that more Hun artillery shells would arrive an hour or so later. The first night there was an attempt to bring food and water up to those in the front lines and to retrieve the wounded. A nearly continuous popping of bright flares produced enough light for the Germans to shell the area; the second night there was no food or water brought up and those wounded during the day had to suffer without aid. Those not wounded also suffered from thirst, hunger and the sounds of the injured.

The men endured in silence; eyes wide opened, on alert while their minds refused to think about all they had seen or even where they were. Those who survived would always remember what Hell looked like.

Doc, Digger and four other members of the squad remained of the twenty that had first gone over the top into the town. After three days in those shallow trenches dug out of the yellow clay beyond the last stone house the men were finally relieved; they moved back through the town. On the ground were bloated bodies of those killed there, nearly all Germans; the Americans and French had been gathered and buried. Doc walked past the piles of those first thirty or so that had surrendered and been fried by the poilu with his flamethrower; the bodies looked like charred cordwood strewn about. One lay on his back with an arm sticking grotesquely up in the air; Doc noticed that doughboys passing by made a point of shaking the hand as they headed up to the front. What would have seemed unbelievable to him a year earlier was now something he merely watched with no emotion. He and his men were directed to a truck which would bring them to a rest area a few miles behind the lines. After the six of them climbed aboard, Doc was the last to fall asleep, taking at most two minutes to do so; oblivious to the German artillery shells exploding nearby.

Hosptial 12

"Miss Rundquist, come in." The Major sat at his desk, a few neat piles of papers in front of him. He stood and motioned for Esther to sit. "The new ward building is complete; a few more days and the equipment, beds and all will be in place. What we need will be the staff; how is their training progressing?"

"Fine, Major; all of the nurses are ready. We could use additional orderlies, but they'll show up with the wounded. Several volunteer to stay and help look after their division mates. We'll manage. I'll be staying in the ward as well for awhile; I've worked with gas patients before, you know."

80

"That will be fine. Now that the hospital is complete, I'm being moved to another that's just been started closer to Paris; be leaving in the morning. It's been a pleasure serving with you. I've wondered if you plan on staying in France when the war is over or if you've a desire to return to your home in Wisconsin."

"Honestly, I've not given it much thought. I've been involved here since 1914 remember; I can barely recall France before there was this war. Four years seems so long. I suppose there'll be plenty of work here, though I'd like to see my family again. It would probably be best for me to go home, rather than ask them to visit here, given the circumstances."

"Certainly; I don't imagine France will be the picturesque destination for travelers for some time to come. Rebuilding a country can't provide much entertainment for tourists. Well, the first boat back won't be too soon for me. But, of course, wherever the Army leads...." He shrugged, the expression of a soldier used to obeying orders.

Esther excused herself and headed down the stairs to the ground level. As she walked out, into the sunshine, she smelled the scent of France in summer. She closed her eyes, trying to remember how it had been when she'd first arrived four years earlier. She could almost bring back the excitement of studying in Paris, the anticipation of it all; the parties, studying in a country so different from her own. She had thought she would fall in love with one of the sophisticated European men who carried a somewhat remarkable name. Truth was she had met a nice French man shortly after arriving in Paris. He had been one of the first casualties in the German invasion of France. Since his death, Esther gave little thought of personal pleasures or the fun she once looked forward to with such abandon. Now she was content to see the war through to its finish and...

The sound of several dozen airplanes interrupted her thoughts; looking up she saw a formation of bombers heading east, to drop their bombs on the enemy. She sighed and turned, heading down the walkway towards the new building; trucks with more wounded were arriving.

Oakview

Roscoe walked to the door of the barn with his head down, a worried look on his face. Sam met him, took one look at the yellow envelope in his hand and called for Jack.

"Mr Weldon, I know these aren't usually good news; I'm sorry it was me had to bring it out to you. It was at Fedder's store and he asked if I'd deliver it. Don't normally handle telegrams, you know."

"Thank you Roscoe. Sam, why don't you go and get Roscoe a cool glass of lemonade; I think Mother just made some up."

"Sure. I'll be right back." Sam walked up to the house, wondering what the envelope contained. As he swung the door to the kitchen open, Phebe asked him if that was Roscoe's truck she'd heard in the drive. He told her of the yellow envelope he'd brought and that Jack wanted a cool drink for the carrier. Phebe's face went pale as she stifled a gasp with the back of her hand. She hurried out the door, telling Sam the lemonade was in the icebox.

Jack's hands were unsteady as he carefully opened the envelope. Phebe was at his side, tears already forming in her eyes. Roscoe stood a respectful distance back, ready to slow or stop Sam when he came in. "Deeply regret to inform you that Corporal Earl Weldon, Infantry, is officially reported as killed in action May 1918. The Adjutant General".

He tried to fold the telegram as his wife dropped her head to his chest. "Jack, oh Jack" was all Phebe kept saying as she sobbed. Sam came around the corner and Roscoe went to him to quietly inform him that Earl was dead. Jack held Phebe for a long time; Sam was sitting on a hay bale, staring at nothing. Roscoe would never forget the scene as he drove the Model T down the drive to the road.

Visitors came by bringing meals and sitting in silence with Jack, Phebe and Sam. A memorial service was held at the Oakview church and a marker placed in the woods near Grandpa Isaiah. The family knew the blessing of friends and neighbors who honestly shared their grief; it's what brought them through, again.

Chapter 20
July 1918

<u>At the Front</u>

"Over the top, men. Let's go. Death to the Huns."

Dautin stepped up the ladder, one of the first in the initial wave to go. A man next to him was hit, six or seven bullets tearing out his back, little geysers of blood starting as he fell in a heap back down on top of others in the trench. Doc pulled his helmet a bit tighter on his head as he went forward, leaning into the lead rain the Germans were sending their way. The regiment was tasked with advancing beyond the road ahead and up a gently sloping ridge about a half mile further on. Their artillery support was late as was often the case; the shells started bursting out in front after a good number of men had already been cut to pieces by the enemy machine guns. At the moment it wasn't even possible to pick out the sound of a single one; the 'put-put-put' of each merging into a chorus of spitting death.

He was crossing a field of beautiful orange flowers which was quickly being uprooted and turned into another black gash that resembled so much of the French countryside he'd been through. He imagined Digger making a snide comment about the supposed beauty of this place and what it was that attracted so many tourists. He hoped his friend had more important things on his mind at the moment. Doc arrived at the near side of the raised roadbed, taking shelter in the three foot high wall it formed between him and the cursed machine guns. He was surprised to find Digger landing next to him at the same moment he hit the dirt.

"What the damn hell are we doing here, Doc?"

"Same thing we do every other day lately, friend. Glad to know we're both alive and kicking. Here, help me with this a second." Doc was slipping his bayonet out of its scabbard, getting ready to raise his helmet above the road level. "Let's see if they know we're here." Lifting it up, he slowly moved it back and forth, with just the top of the helmet showing. A few seconds later it flew off the bayonet, pierced by two bullets, a shower of dirt following it down.

"Yep, Doc; seems they know we're here. Now you won't have to worry about sweating in your helmet, you ought to enjoy the breeze blowing through those holes."

The sound of a new support barrage coming over made them tense up, getting ready to go over the road behind the cover it would provide. Doc looked to his right and saw several men start forward; nobody got shot. The German machine gunners couldn't see through the smoke and dirt of the barrage; or maybe, just maybe, the artillery landed on the damn things and knocked them out.

Over the top went Doc, Digger at his side and what was left of their company. It was an awesome sight to see; hundreds of doughboys advancing at a slow run behind the dirt curtain raised by the artillery. He'd gone about fifty yards when the Maxims began to open up on them again, singing that same 'put-put-put' song he'd learned to hate. Doc felt both of his legs go out from under him as he fell, spinning into a newly formed shell hole. He hit hard, knocking the wind out of him. He tried to get up again; that's when the blow to his lower back and pain in both legs swept over him, sending him into a pool of warm, black silence.

He awoke to gathering darkness, lying on his chest with his nose an inch from the dirt. He couldn't move from the waist down, tried to roll over, looked toward his feet and saw a body on his legs; most of a body, anyway. That's when he heard, faintly, the 'whump' of a gas shell landing somewhere close, outside the hole he was in. He tried not to panic, knowing the gas would settle low to the earth, and he was about as low as possible right now. He wiggled and twisted, pain streaking up his back, as he tried to get into the gasmask bag he was lying on. He caught the faintest smell of it, inhaled long and held his breath, squeezing his eyes shut as tight as he could. Managing to just pull out his mask, he got it on his face as the yellow cloud slid down the sides of the hole toward him. He could feel the burning on his face as he sank back into the quiet blackness.

Oakview

"Do you think Dautin knows about Earl? Could he have been with him?" Phebe had so many unanswerable questions; Jack could only listen and try to calm her fears. Losing a son, even one adopted, was hard. The thought of them together was awful; he tried to comfort her, to explain that they served in different units, probably miles apart from each other. Jack seriously doubted that Doc had even been informed of Earl's death; in all probability Earl had only listed them as family, not his brother in the Army. There was a remote chance Dautin might hear about his brother from someone that knew them both, but that was not likely. In the morning Jack would write two letters; one to Dautin and another to Tom Stratton, seeking more information and asking his friend to look for his remaining son.

At the Front

The black troops were assigned to locate and remove the wounded Americans, along with identifying and marking the dead. As two of them approached the edge of a shell hole they peered down into it. "OK, two dead in here; no need to go down. See the yellow tint on the dirt; that's gas. It's always on the bottom. Let's see what's in the next one there."

"Hold up; the one's got his mask on down here. Might still be alive, may have made it through 'til the gas anyway. I'm gonna go look see."

The man put on his own mask and slid to the bottom of the hole. He kicked the body. Deep in the blackness, Doc saw and felt the lightning of the pain in his hips. He moved to get away from whatever was causing it.

"Hey, got a live one here!!! Get help; I'll start digging his legs out of the dirt. Shit, there's another one, all blown to hell, on top of him, too. Get help, hurry, go!!"

Hospital 12

"Esther, we've got one on the way over. Multiple bullet wounds, possible lower paralysis, gas burns and inhalation, the works. We're going to set him up in a private room; a Sergeant from some special unit or something. A doctor will be here shortly to fill you in more on his condition." The new administrator, another Major, was much more informal than either of his predecessors; Esther somehow preferred the way she had been called "Miss Rundquist".

She began arranging the private room, recently occupied by a Lieutenant Colonel who had been transferred to a hospital in England. This Sergeant must be 'something special' alright, she thought. Hope he's not from Alabama... they all seem to be special, in their own eyes. As she finished the room and was leaving, she overheard an officer asking another nurse where he might find her.

"Over here, Captain. Is this about the new patient we're expecting?"

"Yes, Miss Rundquist? Sergeant Weldon will be arriving shortly. I'm here at the request of Major Roberts, our regimental surgeon. He asked around and was told this hospital, and you in particular, would be the best place for Weldon. The Sergeant is in charge of a unit of instructors; the Major asks that he be cared for here. I've heard he was a personal friend of a French Colonel; kind of a special case. He was found in a shell hole near the Soisson road; shot through both legs but seems he must have put on his gas mask before he passed out. Another man was lying across his back and his legs were buried in dirt. That may be what kept him from bleeding to death overnight. There are some burns on his eyes and mouth; we don't know if he was blinded or not. "

"We'll do the best we can; we have found most of the work is up to the patient. How does he feel about getting better?" Esther knew some gas cases gave up too easily; the stigma of possible blindness and other effects were overwhelming to many.

"Honestly, he hasn't been conscious long; I'm not sure if he's said much at all so far."

"Thank you, Captain. We'll look after him; do all we can."

A stretcher was being lifted down from an ambulance as Esther walked with the Captain out of the building. She stood by as Doc was transferred to a wheeled bed and brought in to his room. The first order of business was to bathe him and change the field dressings that had been applied at the forward aid station. The

86

sponge bath was accomplished by two orderlies, a couple of marines from the Second Division. While they were working Esther overheard a small part of their conversation.

"You sure this is him? He don't look so big to me."

"Sure I'm sure; I went over the top with him on a raid a few months back. You remember hearing about the marine that went missing; they found him a few days later; the one the Huns had tied up and hacked to pieces while they questioned him?"

"Yeah, yeah sure, I remember. So this is the guy that headed up that raid? Jeez, all of us wanted to be in on the first one. Things got a bit more serious after they found that missing guy, though; all of us were a bit crazy for awhile. I went into the Kraut lines a week or so later; our gunny Sergeant had to be forced by the Lieutenant to keep a prisoner alive. I heard of one patrol that cut the hands off six of them they killed and left behind the hands of one they brought back living, too; just to shake up the bastards. That's why the Huns call us 'Teufel Hunden', you know, 'Devil Dogs'."

Esther was shocked. Either these two were gravely mistaken or there were things going on, by American soldiers, which she could not believe. In any case, she felt pretty sure this Sergeant meant trouble; maybe that's why he was given a private room. When the orderlies had finished, Esther began applying new bandages to the bullet wounds on Doc's legs. He was lucky neither leg was broken; the holes would heal quickly. Esther gently cleaned the burns on his face; the blisters from the mustard gas were not too severe and she doubted he had inhaled any by his breathing.

In the darkness Doc could feel hands on the upper parts of his body; he couldn't quite figure out what they were doing. He tried moving his legs but couldn't. Suddenly he felt something near his face, thought someone was taking his mask off. Gas! He grabbed for the hands, felt small wrists in his grip, so small it would be easy to break them. Then he heard, out on the edge of somewhere, the voice; it was like an angel, so soft yet full of authority.

"Let go, Sergeant. You're hurting me; I'm here to help. I'm a nurse in the hospital you've been brought to. I'm only changing the bandages on your eyes. You've been wounded. Lie still and please let go of my wrists."

The voice, so beautiful; he had to let go. He tried to focus his eyes, wanted to look to the side but they wouldn't. "Oh God, not my eyes! Please, not my eyes!" The panic was still building when the angel spoke again, "Sergeant, the burns do not look too bad. I've worked with many patients that have been gassed. We won't know for a week, perhaps longer if your vision will come back. You have to trust us and stay calm."

"Why can't I move my legs? I don't even feel them; please tell me I've still got both legs."

The voice, calmly, tried to comfort him. "Yes, you've still got both legs. You have been shot through them but no bones have been broken. Try again to move them, just a little; still can't? You may have some bruising or pressure on your lower back. I was told you were found under another soldier and your legs were buried in the bottom of the hole. Do you remember anything?"

Doc tried to think. Another soldier; who was next to me when we went over the top?   What was left of the squad all went over together. Who was it?   He tried to remember; it finally came to him.

"Digger!!!"

Chapter 21
August 1918

The angel's voice kept him from slipping over the edge into a pit of depression and despair, every bit as deep and dark as the blackness he'd known that night on the battlefield. Doc hadn't even thought to ask if the angel had a name. At this time all he seemed to have left was the sound of the voice. Other voices had spoken words to him; even in the attempts at kindness their words brought him no comfort. Captain Lewis from the regiment he'd been assigned to stopped by to see how he was doing. Doc's only question was about Digger; the Captain said he was one of the thirty men from the company that were listed as missing after the day at Soisson. Lewis was quick to say that it didn't mean Digger was dead; he could have ended up in a hospital like Doc. There hadn't been enough time to find out about everyone; the division had been fighting every day for two weeks.

Monier visited him one afternoon while he was having his bandages changed. Now a Major, Monier had been in the middle of the most terrible fighting for months. His desire was to die a heroic death as he felt there was nothing to live for with his family all dead at the hands of the hated *Boche*. He just couldn't seem to get in the way of that one bullet with his name on it. He brought the news of Colonel LeBeau's death, though he didn't volunteer the information before Doc had pried it out of him. The news brought by the voices continued to grow worse. Just yesterday another familiar voice had come by with words that drove him to the very brink. Colonel Stratton, his former commander at Fort Snelling, had told him of Earl's death. He tried to soften the blow with greetings from home, but Doc knew there was only one reason he'd visit in person. Earl's body had been recovered but the family had decided to have him buried with his mates in France. That decision, at least, Doc understood and agreed with.

The angel's voice was all he had. It alone kept him going; gently and firmly challenging him that there was a future. The wounds were healing well and feeling was returning to his legs; though they often felt like worms were crawling inside them. When he slept his legs often woke him up, spastically twitching and kicking with a mind of their own. This morning he'd been able to wiggle his toes, expecting some words of emotional praise from the voice. In their place the voice, softly admonished him to try and flex the ankles. Doc had become angry at the voice, asking when it would be satisfied with his efforts. The voice calmly replied it was not important for her to be delighted; it was only necessary for Doc. He picked up on the "her" in the reply and asked if she had a name. A barely discernable chuckle was followed by a quietly uttered "Esther; my name is Esther". The simple answer lifted his spirits that had been crushed by the other voices.

<u>Oakview</u>

Jack drove up and parked on the street in front of Fedder's. He and Sam got out and walked into the store; the smells giving them a welcome, comfortable feeling. Sam dug into his pocket and came out with a dime, heading to the horehound candy jar. Jack smiled at the sight of Old Man Fedder already dozing in his chair in the back corner.

"Morning, Jack. Nice day; hint of rain out there, shore could use a titch. Been way too dry for a spell, huh?"

"Yep, Bill, we could use some rain. An inch right now would be real welcome. Say.... Phebe was wondering if you've got any fresh apples in? She used the last of our dried the other day and wants to make dumplings for the social tomorrow. I know it's a bit early, but..."

"It so happens a guy from down below Winona stopped by just yestiddy and brought about three bushels of a new apple. Said it's a 'Minnesota apple' that ripens sooner; he said he bred 'em special to avoid an early winter. His name's Haralson, something like that; said he'd swing by whenever we needed some. Part of an experiment with the University."

"Yumm, nice.... not too sweet. I'll take a half bushel, along with a pound of coffee. Phebe likes to bake and I swill down the java like no tomorrow."

"Say, Jack. Didn't know quite how to do this.... a telegram came for you this morning. I wasn't feeling good about having Roscoe deliver it this time. Here it is..."

Jack began to feel light headed and his hand began to tremble as he took the envelope. "Please, God, not again." He noticed it was from Tom Stratton and blew a long sigh of relief. "Thanks, Bill, better news than last time. It's from a friend in France, used to command the boys up at Fort Snelling. We served together in Cuba. I'll read it when I get home." He put the telegram in his pocket, paid for the goods and motioned to Sam that they were going.

When they arrived at the farm, Phebe was feeding the chickens. The fat red hens were greedily pecking away around her, making a feathery carpet she seemed to be standing in. As she walked, they moved out of the way without stopping for a second. Jack stayed in the car for a moment admiring the look of his wife. The years of hard work and raising the boys hadn't diminished her beauty one bit. He would remember to bring her a bouquet of wildflowers from the field down by the creek after he'd taken care of extending that fence for the new sheep pen. Another thing to look after; a dozen sheep to go with the goats they added since starting the hogs two years ago. The farm was beginning to look like a kid's zoo at the State Fair or something. He reminded himself how much he liked the goat cheese, smoked ham and looked forward to thick wool socks this winter. Store bought goods, so convenient, didn't hold a candle to hand knitted socks.

Jack got out of the truck and walked up to Phebe. She smiled at the expression in his eyes. "And what are you thinking, Mr Weldon?"

"Watching those hens pecking all over; thought I might get a peck on the cheeks myself." Jack gave her a kiss; as she stepped back Phebe wagged a finger at him.

"These girls just might get jealous of all this attention; after all, they have to share the one rooster in the henhouse."

Jack laughed and then remembered the telegram. "I nearly forgot; Tom Stratton sent a telegram. Bill Fedder was a bit apprehensive about giving it to me; almost as much as I was taking it from him.

91

Thought I'd wait to read it together; I expect its news about Dautin." He opened it and began to read.

"Thought best you hear from me. Dautin wounded, not seriously. In Hospital 12 outside Dannes. Visit yesterday, told of brother. Letter to follow. Tom"

"Oh, Jack. Not both of them; what are we to do? How long does a letter take to get here; I'm not sure I can stand waiting. It doesn't even say how he's wounded. Damn this war anyway."

"Phebe, love; Tom says it isn't serious. By the time the letter gets here, probably next week; why, Dautin could be up around and fine by then. I'm very glad Tom sent this; I don't think I could take Roscoe delivering another telegram. Let's go sit on the porch a bit; I'd like to pray for Dautin and all the boys over there. We'll tell Sam; he's in the house."

Hospital 12

In the week since he'd regained complete consciousness Doc had made good progress in his recovery. His legs continued to heal nicely with no signs of infection in the bullet holes. The nervous twitching had settled down as well as the swelling and pain in his lower back. What remained in question were his eyes. The doctors did not want to hurry the healing of them; despite Doc's anxiousness, they insisted that he wait several more days before the bandages be removed. There was a chance the sudden brightness could affect his vision permanently. Meanwhile, he was allowed to sit up for a few hours at a time now. His polite character had won over the nursing staff and there was never a lack of attention when he needed someone's help to eat or when his leg bandages had to be changed. Still, Doc always saved his kindest words and best demeanor for Esther; he knew by her step when she entered his room. He would spend considerable time imagining what she must look like; undoubtedly she resembled the angel she sounded like.

Esther was not exactly sure what it was that drew her thoughts to Doc so often. There were occasions when she would lose her focus while working with the other patients. When one of the nurses mentioned how nice looking he was, even with his eyes bandaged like they were; Esther caught herself speaking sharply to her. She scolded herself for harboring resentment toward the girl; never before had she felt the least bit angry at the words of the other staff. All the same, she enjoyed the way he seemed to brighten up when she'd come in his room. It was as though he knew it was her and not someone else. He had even begun to smile when she spoke, now that the scars from the burns had nearly healed. And what a nice smile it was...

The day arrived when the bandages were to be removed. Doc could feel the tightness around his eyes; he knew the burns there would take longer to heal than those on his mouth. He heard the now familiar steps as she entered his room.

"Good morning, Esther. I hope you slept well because I hardly got a wink. You are going to be part of this parade, aren't you? Hate to have you miss the unveiling." Doc smiled, a look of hesitant expectation on his face.

"Don't worry about a thing. The doctor should arrive shortly; he will be the one to remove the bandages. I'll be here as well. There may be a couple of others in the room; some new nurses we want to be in attendance so they can learn."

"As long as you're close by, you can invite the whole AEF to watch for all I care."

"What a nice thing to say. Just so you'll know, the doctor will be on your left side when he removes the bandages. The shades will be partly lowered to dim the light in the room. I'll be on the right side nearest the door."

"Thanks, I'll know which way to turn to get my first look. I was afraid I'd not know which is you if my vision's blurred." Doc smiled a bit too wide and grimaced a little at the sharpness he felt near his mouth.

"Well, silly, if you must know. I'm the one without the mustache." Esther giggled, caught herself and felt foolish, embarrassed at the lack of decorum.

"So, maybe I'm not the only one who's glad this day is finally here?"

"What! Look, Sergeant Weldon; you're healing at a good rate. We need to get you out of here, what with other patients lining up

93

for our attention. Naturally, I'm glad you've recovered; I feel that way about all our patients. It's my job, you know."

"Whoa, whoa! Look, I'm sorry. I didn't mean anything, didn't mean to be forward or... I just thought maybe you were happy for .... well, anyway, please forgive me. I guess I'm just a dope or worse. So how long will I be hanging around here after I can see?"

"I imagine a few more weeks; we need to make sure the legs are completely healed and there are no problems with your back. Then you'll be sent back to your outfit. I suppose that's what you want? Go back and butcher some German prisoners...." She felt ashamed for having said it; still couldn't believe anyone was capable of doing the things the marines had spoken of when Doc first arrived.

"Excuse me? What ever gave you the idea I'd do something like that? I mean, it gets pretty rotten out there, but I'd never do anything beyond what's necessary for my mission. I want the war to end, but I don't know what you're talking about. Butchering prisoners? I think you've got me confused with a Hun or worse."

"Well, what about the marines? When you were brought in, I overheard someone who recognized you; he was with you on a raid or something. A missing marine was killed by the Germans. Enemy prisoners were butchered." Esther was confused and angry.

"Look; I led a trench raid, training the marines. It's my job. In the confusion one of them ended up in an enemy trench; I don't know how. He was found a few days later, dead. What the marines did about that I've only heard. By the time the kid was found, I was already training other soldiers."

"Really? I thought; I mean, I didn't want to believe you could, would... oh, I've been a fool. Now I've made you angry. I really am very sorry, Sergeant."

"Hey, it's alright. The war's confusing enough without trying to understand it. I don't suppose you could call me Doc? I really don't think Sergeant is a name I want too much longer. My full name is Dautin, but I'm called Doc by practically everyone over

94

here. Thanks for being here for this morning; I mean it. It'll be easier for me to take... well, if I can't... you know."

Esther laid a hand on his shoulder, gently. "Sure. No other place I'd rather be, really. I'm sure everything will work out. By the way, where in the States are you from? I'm from Wisconsin, a small town north of Chicago, but I came to France to study just before the war and now, here I still am."

"Wisconsin? We're practically neighbors; I live on a nice farm in Minnesota, between St Paul and Rochester. The town nearby is so small it almost doesn't have a name."

The doctor came in followed by a nurse carrying a tray with scissors, bandages and other medical items. Four other nurses also entered and stood around the foot of the bed to observe and learn. The physician greeted Doc and explained what would be happening; that the vision may be fuzzy for a bit. It should clear in a few moments and there would be no further problem. The scabbing from the burns would heal with little, if any, scarring. He began to cut away the bandages slowly, allowing time for Doc's eyes to adjust to the gradual increase in light. Cautioning him to keep his eyes closed when the bandages were finally off, the doctor was just removing the last one. An orderly appeared at the doorway and motioned for Esther. She stepped lightly over to the door, her place next to the bed taken quickly by an eager nursing student. The older woman, with a blotchy face and several missing teeth leaned in close to get a better look.

Doc opened his eyes to the face peering intently at him. Seeing his expression, the doctor quipped, "Son, it's obvious there's nothing wrong with your eyes."

The older student blushed and muttered a soft "Sorry" as she stepped back. Doc looked to his right, toward the light spilling in from the hallway. As she turned to look at him, Esther was silhouetted, back lit. As she returned to the bed Esther smiled and with her usual calm voice said hello. "You are an angel", Doc said as the tears began to flow. The doctor started to explain that his eyes were reacting to the sudden light and air. All the students listened intently. Esther and Doc couldn't have cared less; they were heading off into their own world.

Chapter 22
September 1918

The scabbing around his eyes and mouth had healed, leaving a few very small scars no one would notice. Doc was still bothered a bit with intermittent blurred vision and some weakness in his legs and back though he could tell his strength was slowly returning. What he really wanted to do was go for a walk outside. It was a sunny, warm afternoon when Esther came into his room with a bundle of clothes under her arm.

"Good day, Sergeant Weldon" she said with a sweet smile. "How about taking a stroll? I know a place, real quiet, where we can get a home cooked meal; away from army chow and a sea of folks all dressed in hospital attire."

"That's just what this Doc would order, if anyone cared to listen and obey. My legs feel like they need a good stretch; I bet I could walk to Paris today."

"Well, maybe we'll start with a stroll into the village. Here, put these on while I wait outside." Esther laid the clothes over the back of a chair and closed the door behind her. It took Doc all of three minutes to get dressed and out of his room. The two of them walked out of the ward to the admiring nods of other patients and the smiles of several nurses. As they stepped out into the sunshine, Doc closed his eyes and held his face up to the sky.

"Ahhhh, it's been too long since I've felt warmth like this; feels really good."

They headed east toward the village that was once on the edge of the front area. Doc noticed that there was quite a bit of rebuilding going on; old men and boys scurrying around putting up new houses and making repairs to existing ones. He cupped a hand to one ear and tried to hear the sounds of war.

"I've been so busy getting healed up, I forgot all about the fighting. When did the front move so far away you can't hear it anymore?"

"Oh, the French and their new allies, we Americans, have pushed the Germans back several miles in the past week alone. There's talk that the war will be over soon; maybe before you have to get back to it. That would make me very happy." Esther stopped, turned Doc to face her, reached up and gave him a kiss.

"What, what was that for?" Doc was caught off guard by the kiss. "I mean, that was wonderful, but..."

"Well, I've wanted to do that for some time now. Seems a certain nurse has fallen for a patient; strictly against the rules, you understand. Can't have word of that getting around the hospital after all."

"Really? Mum's the word, Miss. My lips are sealed, at least so far as talking that is." Doc reached around her waist and gave her another kiss, longer this time.

"Alright, Sergeant. We've got a meal ahead and I know you won't want to miss it. Let's pick up the pace a little and stretch those legs. It's not even as far as a country mile, as we'd say back home."

Their walk into the village did them both good. Doc was able to loosen up his lower back until it felt nearly good as new. One of his legs just wasn't strong yet but the other felt great. He was hungry, really hungry, for the first time since the day at Soisson. They ate fresh greens and tender lamb; strong, hot coffee with real cream and pastries. It was a meal for royalty and Doc was sure it hadn't come cheap. When he asked Esther about it, she smiled and said she had helped care for the son of the café owner. He had been wounded months earlier, quite badly. Though he'd lost an arm he had recovered and was back in service, leading a company of invalid guards at a prison camp. The meal was a way for his family to show their thanks to the 'infirmière américaine'. They finished with a bottle of wine, also compliments of their hosts who came over to greet Esther and her friend. She conversed easily with them, explaining that Doc was a special instructor of troops and had been among the first to arrive in France to help defeat the Boche. All of the patrons in the café came over to shake his hand and show their appreciation for his service.

As they were walking back, heads a bit fuzzy after the wine, Doc took Esther's hand and stopped. He was nervous; a fluttering feeling in his stomach that he knew was not from the meal they'd shared. He cleared his throat lightly, looked directly into her eyes and began to speak. "There's something I have to say. It won't be long before I go back into the fighting; I know I'm nearly strong enough. Today has shown me how important it is to finish this thing and I know I can help win the victory. I need to know if I can hope you'll be here when it is done. I want to come back, get you and take you home when I leave."

"That's a fine way to ask a girl such a thing! I'll be here when the fighting stops. But you'd better have a sweeter way of asking in the future. Honestly, didn't your parents teach you anything about girls?"

Doc swallowed hard. "Nope, they never did." For the first time since he'd joined the Army, he had no idea what he was supposed to do next. Esther did; she gave him another kiss. They spent the rest of the walk back to the hospital talking of writing to each other and wondering how long the war could last.

Oakview

Sam ran all the way from town to the farm; it wasn't easy but he knew the letter in his pocket was worth the effort. As he took the steps up the porch three at a time, Phebe was in the doorway, wiping her hands on her apron.

"For heaven's sake, Sam, what could be so important that you'd be all lathered up like a race horse or something? Sit down, have some water and cool off."

"Thanks. I was at Fedder's after school and when he gave me the letter, well, I knew I could get here faster than the wagon. I yelled to them as I ran by. I bet they won't get by our driveway for another half hour or better. Here's the letter; it's got Dautin's name on the return."

98

"Well, after all your hard work getting it there's no point in waiting to open and read it. I'm sure Father won't mind; he's not due in until nearly sundown."

Phebe was careful opening the envelope, though her fingers wanted desperately to rip it open. She began to read.

"Hospital 12, France.
September 14, 1918

Folks,

It's been too long since my last letter but much has happened recently. I was wounded a few weeks ago, but I understand Colonel Stratton has sent you word of that. I'm getting along fine now, still a bit weak but the bandages are off and I can see pretty good. Enough to write a few lines, at least. Don't worry about me. The doctors and nurses here are Americans and they know what they're doing. There's one nurse that's been extra nice; she's about as close to an angel as anyone I've met. Her name is Esther. I'll write more about her later, I hope.

When I was shot, the bullet went clean through both of my legs but didn't break any bone. I fell down into a shell hole, they tell me, and someone else landed hard on top of me. I'm sure it must have been Digger, but I wasn't awake then. Somehow I got my gas mask on, am still not sure how I did that, before I got any gas inside my lungs. The gas burned my eyes and mouth a little but my sight is mostly better now. The food is good, better than in the trenches and I'm sleeping in a real soft bed here. I think I'll be well enough to get back into the fight in a few weeks. I'll try to write more as I have time to now.

Your son,
Dautin"

"Well, he certainly isn't long on words, is he?" Phebe turned as she spoke and wiped a tear away.

"At least he's alright. I can't wait until I'm old enough to fight; I'd like to show the Huns a thing or two."

"Hush, Sam. I'm happy Dautin is safe. I wouldn't want to ever face losing you like Earl. You two are my boys as much as

Dautin. I just want you safe, too. Now, you'd best get your chores done before Father gets here. I'm going to throw something special together for supper to celebrate this letters arrival."

Hospital 12

A week later Doc was discharged from the hospital and provided transportation back to his unit, on the road to Metz. The Allies had been pushing the Kaiser's army back all along the front; toward Belgium in the north and Germany in the east. As Doc waited for the transport that would take him to the train station; he and Esther said their goodbyes. Both promised to write and to meet again, here at the hospital, when the fighting ended. One last kiss, long and full of the love they shared and he was on his way.

The next morning Esther had her own 'marching orders'; she was to help set up a new joint French-American hospital at Brest, on the western tip of France. There were reports, many reports, of a new type of flu beginning to spread. A separate hospital to treat the victims was opening in the hope of containing the sickness. She would be working in administration because of her fluency in both languages. The urgency of the situation was evident in the short time she had to pack and leave; she was to be gone the same afternoon. She dashed off a hurried note to Doc in care of Colonel Stratton, letting him know where she would be. Esther prayed the note would get to him.

Two days later Doc arrived at the regimental office near Haudinville, just south of Verdun. The area he traveled through evidenced what four long years of fighting could do to a landscape. There were no trees left standing and in all directions the earth was scoured and punctuated with shell holes of all sizes. Doc was told the land looked like this for many miles to the north where the old forts of Verdun had witnessed the deaths of a million or more men over the course of the war. The vehicle he was in drove by a huge field of fresh graves. The driver explained that the French were making a national cemetery for them; when it was finished it would be more than a thousand acres in size. They both wondered how many would fit in an area that big. In a few minutes the driver announced they were coming to their destination. As he stepped down out of the truck's cab, another transport pulled up alongside. A familiar voice called his name; Doc turned and a huge smile erupted on his face. It was Digger!

The two had a joyful reunion, unmindful of what anyone thought about two doughboys hugging on a street corner.

"Where in the hell have you been? I saw you cut down and blown into a shell hole with another dog face. That was just before a Hun grenade blew up at my feet. I'm missing a pretty good chunk of my butt; hurts to sit down now. Guess I'll be on my feet the rest of this war. I couldn't get any news from anybody at the hospital I was at. They kept saying they didn't have time to find out about one soldier when thousands were dead or wounded. I finally decided I was well enough to travel so I hitched a ride; been standing up the whole way, too."

"Digger, I was sure it was you that ended up on top of me in that hole. They never did tell me who it was; they said with no head, they couldn't be sure who it was. Come on, let's check in and we'll talk on the way back to our unit. I'm anxious to get this damned war over with; I'll tell you a bit about an angel I met and plan on finding again when we're done with the Germans."

"Now don't that beat all. It's just like you, Weldon, to be with a gal the whole time I'm stuck laying face down on a cot in a hospital hallway with my butt up in the air for the world to see."

Chapter 23
October 1918

Doc was truly impressed. The new weapon in his hands would surely help end the war. Long but well balanced, it fired a bullet with the stopping power needed. The Lieutenant that was demonstrating it was the son of the inventor and really knew the gun. It was called the Browning Automatic Rifle but was already known as the B. A. R. With a twenty shot clip it gave enough suppressing fire to keep the Huns' heads down so a unit could maneuver. Doc's commanding officer, now Major Lewis, had been able to procure eight of the weapons for the squad.

"Sergeant Weldon; with this gun replacing the *Chauchat,* we'll be far more effective in the open field. You've heard that most of the Americans are fighting north of here, up towards Sedan. Our job is to hold as many Germans down here as we can, near Metz, to prevent them from moving north. With small units like yours equipped with automatic weapons, we can convince the Hun that we outnumber them down here."

"Yes, sir. A day on the firing range to practice and we'll be ready for action. Digger, let's get the boys out to the range; Christmas presents have arrived early this year."

<u>Brest</u>

Esther was alarmed at the numbers of patients who were not responding to treatment on the wards. Normally the flu would pass through an area making people ill and leaving a handful of dead in its wake, mostly the old and very young. This sickness was attacking healthy, middle aged people and killing a high percentage. Yesterday she had read a report from a German hospital, captured in the allied drive near Belgium showing the same type of infection and a similar mortality rate. Not since the plagues of the Middle Ages had anything this fierce been seen in Europe.

"Mlle Rundquist, une lettre est arrivée pour vous."

Esther thanked the messenger and looked at the letter; it was from her home in Wisconsin. She sat in a chair in the hallway and began to read it. Tears came as she read the news of the death of her mother and brother from flu. Her father wrote that it had struck all the family; that he and her sister were feeling better now. Neighbors and the local church had taken care of the funeral arrangements of her family and another dozen, some of whom she knew, had also died from it. Esther felt an immediate, intense homesickness. She had to go to be with her father and sister.

Hurriedly explaining her need to be with family to the Hospital Administrator and expressing her desire to return as soon as she could, Esther went into her office and wrote a letter to Doc. She told him what had happened and that she planned on being back in France by the end of the year; hopefully the war would end and they could celebrate Christmas together in Paris. She included her home address in Wisconsin so he could write her there and assured him of her continued love and prayers for his health and safety.

Esther spent the afternoon arranging passage on a ship bound for Boston the next morning. While at the ticketing office she picked up a copy of a week old Washington paper. She read of the influenza pandemic in the United States and was shocked that she had not heard of the scope of the spread of it. Reports of thousands of deaths across the country filled the headlines. As she read the paper, a voice addressed her by name. She looked up to see Colonel Stratton standing in front of her.

"Good afternoon, Colonel. What a surprise to see you here."

"Hello Miss Rundquist. You're a long way from your hospital yourself. It happens I've been called to Boston for a briefing. Are you also traveling home?"

"Yes, Colonel; some of my family have died of influenza and I need to be with them and help however I can. I miss them desperately." Esther was on the verge of tears at this point; Colonel Stratton sat down next to her, tenderly took hold of her hands and spoke.

"Miss Rundquist, I do understand. You see, I received word of my own wife's death from this sickness a week ago. I plan on traveling to her grave after my meetings. If there's anything you need while back in the States, get hold of me through the Army. They'll know where I am. Are you planning to stay at home or will you be returning to France? The war is nearly won and we'll need your experience here after the fighting is over. It will take quite some time to get all our boys back home, I'm sure."

"I'm planning on returning soon, Colonel. I've become quite attached to a certain soldier we both know." Esther smiled at the thought of Doc.

"You mean you and young Weldon? Did he ever mention that his father and I fought together in Cuba during the last war? We've been friends, not really close, for years. I don't imagine I'll have the chance of seeing his parents; but if I do I'll give them a good report about you." The Colonel smiled, stood and shook Esther's hand. "I hope to see you on board the ship after we sail. Dinner together with the ship's Captain, perhaps?"

"I'd enjoy that very much, Colonel. Thank you, and thank you ever so much for the comforting words. I'm sorry about your wife. It seems war and disease has touched us all."

"Indeed; but neither will beat us. Until later, Miss."

In the Field

"Mail Call, Sergeant. One for you from a hospital here in France; just picked it up at company HQ."

"Thanks Private." Doc took the envelope and caught the briefest scent of Esther's perfume. He smiled as he opened the envelope and began to read her letter, surprised that he hadn't known she was no longer at Hospital 12. Now she was on her way back to the States; he'd have to write to the Wisconsin address and tell her how sad he felt that she'd lost so much of her family. At the same time, he felt a rising fear for his own parents back home. How bad were things there? He had heard that influenza was going through the army; so far it hadn't gotten to this part of France. Doc took out pencil and paper and began to write to Esther. He'd finish and post it right away, before tonight's mission.

Oakview

Sam's fever continued; Phebe used everything she'd learned to try to bring it down closer to normal. His breathing was labored and sounded like the dry leaves of autumn corn stalks rasping together. Doctor Phillips had been called for from town; he was out on another house call but would come over as soon as he returned. Phebe heard of several other cases of influenza in the area and so far everyone had overcome the illness. She continued to bathe Sam's face and neck with a mixture of water and alcohol and made sure the mustard poultice on his chest was fresh. It was all she knew.

The doctor arrived just before first light; he looked as though he'd aged a decade in the past week. As he came into the room and looked at Sam the expression on his face told Phebe the worst was ahead. He listened to the boys breathing while he checked his pulse. Turning to her, he shook his head at the same moment Jack walked in from finishing the morning milking. Phebe's shoulders heaved as she muffled the first sobs with the back of her hand. Jack leaned over from behind and hugged her, trying with all his own strength to comfort his wife. He looked at Doc Phillips and asked, "How long does he have?"

"Can't say for certain; an hour, perhaps two. Not long." Phillips sat down hard in the chair by the door and lit a cigarette. "Sam's the third tonight; I'd thought it was passing out of the area without anyone dying. I was wrong; it may be we're only at the beginning. I've spoken with other doctors in the area, even the Mayos over in Rochester and others up at the University. They don't have any answers as yet. They say it's practically everywhere in the country and is even worse in Europe. After all those people have suffered with the war, now this." He snubbed out the cigarette, stood and stretched. "I've got two more stops I know of before another day starts. I'll see myself out. I only wish there was more...."

"We know, Doctor. We appreciate all you do for us and everyone in Oakview. You delivered Dautin, remember? Middle of the night, lightning everywhere, a twister went through between here and Northfield. You do more than fifty other doctors. Thanks."

As Jack walked with the doctor to the door, Phebe handed him a basket with fresh baked bread and homemade cheese. With tears in her eyes she said, "Yes, thank you ever so much. I'll be praying for your own strength through this."

Jack and Phebe sat at the foot of the bed for the rest of Sam's short life, holding his hands and praying that he would enter his eternal rest peacefully. The boy never struggled; his breathing slowed and his lips formed a smile. Barely audible, he whispered "It's pretty", and was gone.

In the Field

"Digger, over there, on the left.... did you see that? They're coming around the left, there.... behind that old foundation."

"OK, Doc, we got it." Digger and one of the new guys, Thompson, quietly shifted and rolled over the top of the crater's edge and slipped into another a few yards away. Their movement didn't draw any fire from the German lines, barely sixty feet in front. Doc and the other two men still with him each drew a grenade out, pulled the primers and threw them over where the Germans had been seen. The three explosions set off a cacophony of gunfire in response; Doc knew they were heavily outnumbered and dawn was getting closer. If they were stuck out here when the sun came up, things could get pretty bad in a hurry.

He could just see Digger's helmet in the next shell hole and threw a pebble that bounced and hit his friend. Digger turned to look; Doc signaled for him to back out and head for their own lines. He watched as the two exited their hole and crawled to the west. They had barely left their shelter when a German potato masher grenade arced into it and exploded. Doc blew a sigh of relief and signaled his own two comrades to follow Digger. Doc hung back long enough to provide a bit of covering fire from his B.A.R. before leaving. He could hear the 'put-put-put' of a Maxim behind him and saw dirt kicking up just to his right moving his way. He rolled to the left and felt bullets tugging at his shirt; one left a burning streak on his upper back. A soldier ahead of him, he wasn't sure which in the dark, pitched up with a sudden jerk, letting out a soft cry before slumping, motionless.

Minutes later they were back in the relative safety of a friendly position. Digger was already lighting up, offering a match to Thompson. Doc counted only one man missing; McIntosh, a young kid from up north near Superior. He walked into the company commander's tent to make his report. His new Captain, another youngster from West Point looked so fresh and clean in his tailored uniform. Doc stated what he saw out front; the Germans had reinforced their position with, perhaps, another full company. That was what they wanted; more Germans here meant less where the main attacks were going forward. His reporting finished, Doc and Digger found a comfortable spot to grab some 'shut eye' before the sun came up. Digger's comment about "just another night's work" was the last thing Doc heard before drifting off to sleep.

When he woke up Doc saw Digger playing with a coin; flipping it over and over again, all the while softly chuckling and wearing a silly grin. When he asked his friend if he was feeling alright, Digger answered, "What? Yeah, I'm fine; just thinking of what fun I can have with this thing. It's a two headed half dollar my brother sent me while I was in the hospital. Never lost a bet while I was there; you just gotta get a guy to 'flip for it' and you're on the way to the bank."

"Sounds just like something a guy from Brooklyn would think up. You really think folks in Abilene will fall for it?"

"Awww, I'm thinkin' of moving around when I get back to the States. I've seen enough flat land for a lifetime anyhow. Maybe live in the mountains somewhere; what about you, Doc?"

"I'm pretty sure I'll be taking over the farm in Minnesota from my folks. Esther comes from Wisconsin, that's only a day or so away. It's hard to think about what comes after the fighting stops, if it stops. I know we've got the 'Hun on the run' right now; I'll decide when I wake up and don't hear guns firing anymore, I suppose."

Boston

"Colonel Stratton, I want to thank you for a most enjoyable voyage. I've truly appreciated not being reminded constantly of the war and the suffering. I do hope your meetings in Boston help to bring all this madness to an end quickly."

"Miss Rundquist, how long do you plan on staying at home, if I may ask? The war is winding down; there will still be a need in France for your services, as I've said before. I know I'll be returning in a few weeks; any chance of our traveling back on the same ship again?"

"I couldn't say, Colonel. I'll be in Wisconsin day after tomorrow, if the trains run on time. A few weeks doesn't sound like long enough, though I'll know more when I get home. How about I send you a telegram, after I find out the situation and decide what to do?"

"Fine. Let me write down the address I'll be staying at for the conferences here. It would be a much more enjoyable trip back with you at the Captain's table again. Until later, Miss."

The ship's steward called a taxi for Esther to drive her to the train station. She thought about taking the time to enjoy a day in Boston but the desire to be with the remainder of her family spurred her on. The train left a half hour after she arrived at the station, barely giving her time to settle in to her compartment. With the government Railway Administration running the transportation service nationwide, she was allowed a separate berth. She was a little surprised to find that working for an Army hospital granted her a bit of privilege. Esther enjoyed sitting in a dining car, watching the scenery rush by the windows between the cities as the train made its way west. There were no wrecked villages or fields ruined by artillery fire; no splintered remains of once beautiful woods along the trip. The wonderful fall colors here reminded her of what France should look like. She saw no evidence of the war, except that most of the other passengers were in military uniform and seemed less relaxed than herself. Esther felt there was a sense of apprehension; people seemed almost afraid to get close. Many wore gauze masks that reminded her of the world wide effect influenza was having.

Esther was greeted at the station in Madison by her father and sister, Milly; many tears were shed, both in sadness over their loss and in gratitude for being together again. It had been more than four years since they had seen one another and the two hour long drive home was full of sharing stories. She told them of Dautin; how they had met at the hospital and their love for each other. Her father was glad for her happiness; expressing his hope that their future together would be as full of love as his own had been with her mother. Milly wanted to know all about him and was surprised and disappointed that Esther didn't even have a picture of him.

They stopped at the house for a short time, getting Esther settled in her old bedroom; flooding her mind with happy memories of her childhood. Part of her felt she could stay forever, not return to the carnage and disease in Europe. In her mind, a small voice reminded her of her commitment and promise to return soon; a promise to meet the love of her life over there when the fighting ended. After putting things away they headed across town to the cemetery. A few cousins joined them there, greeting one another in hushed tones and somber spirits. The sickness had hit more than her immediate family; she noticed too many freshly dug graves for a small town. The war and flu had cost the town dearly and left behind feelings of sadness like a thick fog. Esther thought about Doc's family; wondered if she had the time to travel further and meet them. One day she would and vowed to herself that it would be a happy time; happier than her own reunion here at home.

In the Field

"Sergeant Weldon, come in. I have a most unusual order here for you; one of pride to take part in. You're to report for immediate transit to Boston; the ship leaves from Brest tomorrow afternoon. You'll be sailing aboard a fast escort ship with several others to be an honor guard for Brigadier General Stratton. I'm told he took sick during a war conference and is to be buried at a .... ummm, Fort Snelling cemetery, back in Minnesota. You'll be traveling with his staff who will be the rest of the honor guard. You're to be granted two weeks after the burial before you report back to Fort Upton in New York for further assignment. After reading this, I don't expect to see you here again, unless the war really heats up again. Word is, the Kaiser is about to throw in the towel and we'll all be done in a few more weeks. I hate to see you gone with the end so close, but orders are orders. I never met the General, of course he was a Colonel when he left for the conference; sad how he died just a few days after his promotion."

"He was a personal friend of my father; they fought together in Cuba back in '98. I was under his command when I first enlisted two years ago, though it seems longer than that. If that's all, sir, I'd best get packing if I'm to meet a ship in Brest by tomorrow."

"Yes, yes; I'll arrange a driver. This is quite a surprise and an honor for you. Be back here in a half hour; the driver will be here."

Doc's head was whirling; he half expected to wake up and find out this was a dream. He headed back to his tent and found Digger there. This wasn't going to be easy, to say goodbye to his best friend. Digger had already heard about Doc's orders; again, the guy involved was about the last to find out.

"So when does the taxi pull up to take you home?"

"The Captain said I've got a half hour to pack and get over to Company HQ. We've a bit of time to talk, I guess."

"You have any idea when you'll be back? I heard you'll get some time in the States after Stratton's funeral; think there's a chance to see your folks?"

"I'm sure they'll be at the funeral; it's at Fort Snelling. That's only a few hours from the farm, less than 75 miles. My dad and the Colonel, I mean the General, were good friends in Cuba. Too bad Colonel LeBeau isn't around; he'd be there, too. Anyway, I'd better pack up and get ready to leave."

"Here, I want you to have this." Digger was holding out the double-headed coin his brother had sent him. "Consider it a good luck piece; never know when you might need some on your trip. I'll get my brother to send me another one."

"Really? Thanks. Don't know what I'll use it for but in a pinch it'll probably pay for a sandwich or something. Listen, I want you to keep your dumb head down out there. This thing is almost over; I can feel it. Get home in one piece and we'll run into each other."

"Sure. Keep your feet dry 'crossing the pond' yourself; still those damned submarines out there. What are you going to do about Esther? Do you have time to go see her on your way out of France?"

"I got a letter from her last week; she's back in the States herself by now, in Wisconsin. Her family got hit really hard by influenza. I'm going to go find her, it's not far. Strange how this is playing out, huh?"

110

"Yeah, you always had pretty good luck. Say, maybe you don't need that coin after all?" Digger held out his hand with a smile on his face.

"Not a chance; already tucked away nice and safe....."

Chapter 24
November 1918

<u>Oakview</u>

The military car drove up the drive and parked near the house. Jack heard it approaching and was out of the barn waiting as it stopped; his breath creating vapors in the frosty morning air. This was very strange, yet he had a peaceful feeling about it, like it wasn't about his son. A soldier got out, stretched a little and said, "I'm looking for Captain Weldon? Where might I find him?"

"Well, I haven't been called that in quite awhile. I'm Jack Weldon." As Jack held out his hand, the Lieutenant had a puzzled look on his face.

"Yes sir. I mean Mister Weldon. I'm Lieutenant Hawkins from Fort Snelling; I've been sent with a message for you, Captain..., excuse me, MISTER Weldon. Can we go inside?"

"Sure; sorry, Lieutenant.... bad manners on my part. It's much nicer in the house. Care for something? Coffee, maybe? Must have been an early start to get here before morning's over. Let's see what my wife might have on the stove..."

Jack led the way into the house. The kitchen was nice and warm on this brisk November morning. Jack took the officer's coat and was hanging it up when Phebe walked in.

"Jack? Did I hear a car come in.... oooh, excuse me." She wore a very worried look on her face and appeared about ready to burst into tears. Jack quickly reassured her that everything was alright.

"Honey, this is Lieutenant Hawkins, down from Fort Snelling. He has a message for me about...?"

"Oh, yes sir. My apologies for not getting right to the point outside, Captain. I'm to inform you that Brigadier General Stratton has passed away in Boston. Arrangements are being made for his burial at Fort Snelling. The General, just before he died, made a request that you be asked to assist as part of the ceremony, sir. It's scheduled for the eleventh of this month, a week from today. We will have a driver down a few days before to pick up you and Mrs Weldon. We have a room reserved for you at the Fort."

"Tom Stratton is dead? In Boston?"

"Yes sir. He was attending a military conference when he took ill; influenza is pretty bad on the east coast."

"Excuse me." Phebe was dabbing her eyes with a handkerchief as she turned to leave the room. Jack gave her a loving look as he spoke to the Lieutenant.

"We know about influenza; lost a son to it two weeks ago. Our oldest boy is in France and another was killed there months back. It's been a pretty rough year."

"I'm sorry to hear that, Mister Weldon. I lost my older brother at Château-Thierry in July."

"Sit down, Lieutenant. Let's go over the details for next week; Tom Stratton and I fought in Cuba together. We were pretty close then. He was a good soldier."

The two spent a half hour as Hawkins explained to Jack what his part would be in the funeral ceremony for his friend. When they were done, the officer excused himself and said he felt it best to decline Jack's offer of lunch. He would eat on his way back to Fort Snelling. Jack walked him out to his car and watched as the young man drove away; thoughts of Dautin filled his mind as he went back into the house to comfort Phebe. He also began to think of who to ask about watching the farm while they were away.

Wisconsin

Esther felt a bit uneasy, like she was a stranger that didn't quite fit in. Her father and sister, even her cousins and other family, had been through their own hard times lately. Influenza had taken many of them; the rest had all relied heavily on each other to get over the past months. She was sure they didn't mean to treat her like an outsider; it simply happened. As hard as she tried there

113

was a shell of togetherness, of survival, that surrounded them; it kept them together and her on the outside. After a week at home she had made up her mind to return to France where she fit in; there she had purpose. Esther sent a telegram to Colonel Stratton at the Boston address he'd given her. In it she told him of her intention to sail back to Europe together. That afternoon she told her father and sister of her decision. They said it was fine, that they understood and would be okay. Her sister was no longer a child and was taking good care of her father.

She booked a train ticket to the coast; her father and sister drove her back to Madison. This time the car ride was quieter, with little conversation beyond polite talk. There were hugs and kisses at the train station and almost a sense of relief at the goodbyes. Even Milly seemed resigned to the idea that, for awhile, life would not hold any real joy. It hurt Esther to think that her own family was another casualty of the times. As she settled into her berth, a warm feeling, too warm, came over her and a tightening in her chest followed the first dry cough.

On the Atlantic

Jack remembered his initial crossing as a lot smoother; he didn't understand how different sailing would be on a smaller ship. The fast destroyer taking him to the States bobbed and weaved with sudden, often violent jumps and twists. Several of the officers on General Stratton's staff were in their berths suffering from seasickness. The only discomfort Jack felt was a lack of appetite; the food just didn't appeal to him, despite how good it looked. He smiled at the memory of the first meal with the staff in the wardroom before they left Brest harbor. One young staff Captain had looked over Jack's uniform and commented on his medals, asking him about his Croix de Guerre, the medal for valor in the French army, with two bronze stars attached. Doc quietly explained he had been awarded the medal on three separate occasions. From that point on no one questioned his place in the upcoming funeral proceedings.

The trip across the Atlantic took less than half the time of his earlier voyage. The destroyer traveled alone and was too fast for submarines to effectively challenge. The ship docked in Boston harbor and the staff officers, including Doc, were quietly taken to the train station to continue the trip to Minnesota by rail. Doc was amazed at how quickly they had traveled a quarter of the way around the world.

As they boarded the train each man was given a gauze mask to wear; this was to help prevent them from catching the flu virus. They were told that a second wave of the disease had passed through several large cities, including Philadelphia where 4,000 people had died from it since September. The men were astounded that they had heard nothing of the pandemic hitting the United States. They knew of soldiers getting sick in France; to them that was simply another problem associated with trench warfare and the crowded unsanitary conditions. One of the officers picked up a copy of a New York paper; there were no articles at all about the influenza problem. They dutifully put on the masks; within an hour all had removed them after noticing a Majority of passengers on the train were not wearing any. Because of the lack of a national policy, the pandemic was handled by individual states and cities; some were stricter than others in enforcement of public gatherings, school closing and other social attempts to limit the spread of the disease. Because some cities actually forbade people traveling within their areas, the train seldom stopped; this allowed a much faster trip to St Paul.

When they arrived, the officers and Doc were met at the station by transport from Fort Snelling. They were told there would be no opportunity to leave the Fort's compounds during the time of their stay. Doc was not sure how that would impact his plans to visit Oakview after the funeral. He would try to find an answer to that question in the day left before the burial. After unpacking in a visitor's room, Doc headed over to the main administration offices. On the way he spotted a couple walking together by the officers' club. There was something familiar in the way they strolled hand in hand. Doc quickened his pace; as he closed the distance between them, he recognized his father's dress coat. Breaking into a run, Doc called to them. Phebe stopped and turned at the sound of her son's voice. With a delighted squeal she was caught by Doc and spun around, feeling like a schoolgirl. Her tears of joy moistened his cheek as they hugged. Jack waited his turn, and then pumped his son's hand as he gave him a hearty slap on the back. The two began to rapidly fire questions at each other as they continued walking. Phebe relished strolling with both hands held by her men.

Dinner together that evening capped off a day of animated conversation. Moments of shared sorrow as Doc learned of Sam's recent death and their first chance to grieve the loss of Earl were interspersed with the joyful revelation of Doc and Esther's growing relationship. Jack pulled several humorous tales out of his son as well; knowing that a soldier's life is full of comic adventure, usually at the expense of a comrade. Doc showed them his 'lucky coin' while telling about Digger and others he had come to know in the training and fighting. It seemed their combined stories were enough to fill an entire lifetime when, in reality, they had been apart only eighteen months.

"Tell me more about Esther, son. Have you made plans to visit her family while you're back here on leave? Is there a chance she is still home with her father and sister? Perhaps she could even arrange a short visit with us?" Phebe looked forward to the chance, any real chance, of a genuine female presence; she had been surrounded by only men and boys for too long. She loved her life, and her men, but longed for another woman to talk with each day.

"I don't know, mother. I only received the one letter from her about coming to see her family in Wisconsin; that was just days before I got my own orders. I could try calling her; I don't even know if they have a phone. I thought I'd send a telegram tomorrow. Did you know that the Army is not allowing us to even leave the Fort until the influenza passes through? We were told that when we arrived; so I'm not sure I could go to Esther even if I find out where's she's at or how long she'll be there. Right now I'm here with my parents and that's what I'll enjoy." He raised his glass, looked into his father's eyes and said, "To the Weldon family."

Jack and Phebe smiled and raised their glasses as well.

On the Train

Esther was not at all well; she still had the presence of mind to know she had to get off the train and into a hospital somewhere. She had retired to her berth and notified the porter that she was ill, probably with influenza. The porter was able to make arrangements for Esther to be taken from the train when it stopped near New York City. Here the Red Cross picked her up and transported her to a hospital close by. It was the last thing

116

she remembered for days to come as the sickness attacked her with its unrelenting fever, aches, coughs and chills. There was grave doubt, on the part of many of the doctors and nurses, whether Esther would survive.

The pandemic's second wave had crashed upon the cities of the United States with the power of a tidal wave. Philadelphia was not alone in the grips of it; many thousands of people were dying in North America, millions around the world. As the Great War in Europe was in its final weeks, a new enemy arrived; one that didn't chose sides but attacked everyone and everywhere without remorse. In the final years of the last century, doctors and scientists had learned much about diseases like this one; how they began and a little about how they spread. What they hadn't learned, and still didn't know, was how to effectively treat it or keep it confined. Populations were used to outbreaks of smallpox, typhus and influenza in isolated areas. With the increased movement of millions of people because of the World War, this outbreak was not isolated; it traveled with the soldiers and refugees to all corners of the globe. History would come to learn that this was worse than The Plague or Black Death of Europe in the Dark Ages. The final death toll would exceed the numbers killed in the War.

Fort Snelling

The funeral of newly promoted Brigadier General Thomas Stratton was a somber affair. The weather cooperated fully; gray, leaden clouds scudded across the sky carried by a damp and chilling northwest wind. The few snowflakes falling were driven almost horizontally by it. A caisson with his flag covered casket was pulled by four white horses, each draped in black from nose to tail. Behind marched his honor guard, including Dautin, along with a smattering of other officers and friends; everyone was bundled up against the cold wind. The Fort's chapel had seen a memorial service that comprised talks by several senior officers who had served with Stratton throughout his career. Perhaps the most moving was that given by Jack Weldon, who had served with him in their younger days in Cuba twenty years earlier. Jack recounted several of the spirited escapades that included men like Winston Churchill and Henri LeBeau. Some were still around; others along with LeBeau and Stratton were gone. Jack emphasized what all of them had in common; besides a taste for fun was a genuine and abiding patriotism. Coming from different countries, they shared the same spirit of affection and loyalty.

Now it was Dautin's turn to honor the General. Along with the former staff, he carried Stratton's casket to its final resting place. The skies opened up with heavy snow as he was laid in the ground. Afterward Dautin, Jack and Phebe were invited by the staff to join them in the Officer's Club. As they walked across the compound to the Club, church bells from Minneapolis began to ring, joined by sirens on the base and hundreds of soldiers running out of the barracks. All of them were laughing, shouting and throwing hats into the air. Some ran by yelling that the war was over; the Kaiser had abdicated and was in exile. The Allies had won! Dinner was a joyous affair, the gloom over their friend's death put aside with the overwhelming news of peace. Several glasses were raised in toasts to the General and victory for the United States.

Dautin's parents had decided to travel part of the way back home that very night; they were concerned about being away from the farm for this long. They had left the place in the care of a friend, but still felt it best to be leaving. They hoped to find a room somewhere along the road, perhaps around Hastings. The Army didn't feel it had the authority to require civilians to remain in the Fort's environs during the influenza threat. Jack and Phebe were hopeful that Dautin would be able to come down to Oakview for a visit before his two weeks of leave expired. A telegram was waiting in Dautin's room when he returned from seeing them off. He opened the yellow Western Union envelope and read:

"Dautin,
Esther's visit over. Left on train two days ago for Boston. On ship for France leaving 15th. Good luck. Hope to meet one day. Elmer Rundquist."

She was leaving November 15th! He had three days to get to Boston and meet her before she sailed. But he couldn't leave the Fort; at least he didn't think so. He would have to get an answer first thing in the morning; it was too late an hour now. The train they had taken here from Boston had made the run in two days. If he could get aboard another heading east, he could just make it. Dautin's mind was racing, trying to figure out what he should do. If he was stuck here because of the quarantine, he'd miss her for sure and would have to travel all the way to Europe to find her.

With the war over, the odds of the Army allowing him to do that were, no doubt, getting smaller every day. He couldn't imagine they would continue to send men over; they'd be starting to get them back here to the States as soon as possible. He tried writing a telegram to Esther but had no idea where to send it. He couldn't phone his folks; they wouldn't be back until tomorrow afternoon and that would be too late to leave for Boston. At least he knew there was no point in thinking about a trip to Wisconsin; Esther was no longer there. He pondered the situation and all the obstacles between himself and his love; frustrated that nothing could be done in the middle of the night. First he would get permission to leave the Fort, then book a ticket on the next train to Boston. The whole thing started poorly as he didn't sleep a wink all night.

At six o'clock the next morning Doc was knocking on the door of Major Williams, the senior officer from General Stratton's former staff. The Major listened to Doc's story, shook his head and expressed surprise that the young man would think there was any chance of success for this mission he was contemplating.

"Sir, please. Haven't you ever been in love? If I don't go get her now, before she leaves for France, I'll probably never find her again."

After several minutes of listening to Doc's plan the officer finally relented. He smiled and said, "Hell son, with the war over this might just be the most worthwhile job I've got left to do. You go see if there's a train schedule in the Admin Office; I'll get up Lieutenant Saunders. He's the most reckless man I know when it comes to automobiles, just the person we need to get you to the station quick like."

Doc ran all the way to the Admin building and found a clerk who knew about the train schedules. If there were no changes, an express was supposed to leave for Fort Upton in about two hours; that should allow him time to get to the station before it headed out. The problem was the quarantine; no one was allowed off base until the duty officer was informed otherwise. Doc ran back to the Major's quarters where he found Williams and Saunders dressed and ready to go. Doc explained the dilemma of the quarantine; the Major assured him he'd get around that. The three went back to the Admin Office and found the duty officer, a Captain.

119

"Good morning, Captain. I have business in St Paul and will need to leave the base for a few hours. I'll be bringing along my aide and driver."

"Sorry, Major. No can do, sir. Orders are no one leaves until we get word from the State Adjutant's office at the Capitol."

"Look son. We have an emergency of sorts that we need to work on, very important. How about we promise not to come within 20 feet of anybody on the way, so we don't catch the damned flu? You a gambling man, Captain? How about we flip a coin? Heads we go, tails we don't. Sergeant, you had some change in your pocket last night, right? Get a coin out we can flip."

"Yes, sir. Right here, Major." Doc glanced at Lieutenant Saunders, who was feigning the most serious expression at the moment. Doc tossed the coin in the air; unless it had landed on its edge, there was no losing this bet.

"Heads, I knew I'd get lucky. Sorry Captain, looks like we'll be heading out. Be back by noon."

The three men left the Captain standing in his office wondering what had just happened. He didn't even know who the three were; he'd never seen them at the Fort before. He walked over to the ringing telephone on his desk, shrugged and picked it up.

Step one of 'Operation Esther' was a success. Now they had to get Doc to the train station before the express left. Saunders drove like he was Barney Oldfield; weaving and passing cars on the old Fort Road. Fortunately, it was already the quickest way to the station in downtown St Paul; it had been the main route since it was a walking path back in the middle 1800's. They arrived with more than a half hour to spare. Doc bought his ticket, the express was still scheduled to get to Fort Upton early on the 14th. That would give him a full day and half of the 15th before the ship left Boston. The railway clerk assured him there was a connecting train that could get him there in time. Doc shook hands with Major Williams and Lieutenant Saunders and thanked them heartily. He also handed them a letter to post; it was to his folks in Oakview explaining what he was trying to do. Doc grabbed his kit from the backseat of the auto and headed into the station. Behind him he heard the Major saying, "Look Saunders, you ever drive like that

120

again with me in that infernal contraption and I'll have you peeling potatoes for a month. Good job."

"Where, where am I?" Esther woke in a very familiar setting; except she was in the bed, not standing and attending a patient. She looked around at the undecorated walls, the tiled floor and small plain cupboard with a wash basin on it. It was definitely a hospital room, but it could have been in Chicago or anywhere in the world so far as she knew.

"Miss Rundquist, is it? We got your name from the train porter when the ambulance crew picked you up. Do you remember leaving the train?" The nurse was a supervisor, like herself. She had never before known what it was like to be on the receiving end of nursing.

"No, not really. I was not feeling at all well; fever, aches and all of it. I'm thinking it's the flu; I saw plenty of it in France."

"France? When were you there? We got you off the train near Fort Upton; it was an eastbound run I believe."

"Yes, that's right. I'd been home in Wisconsin visiting my family. Have to board a ship back to the war from Boston on the 15th..... my goodness! It's not already past the 15th is it? I simply can't miss the ship; and I'll have to write my father a letter to let him know what's happened."

"Settle back, you don't want to get all worn out, do you? Today is the 12th of November; I don't know about getting to Boston by the 15th. You're in no condition to travel and besides, with the war ending yesterday, I'm not sure you'll be heading over there anyway."

"What? The war ended yesterday? But I'm supposed to meet Colonel Stratton in Boston; we're sailing back to France. I'm needed at the hospital in Brest. I was only supposed to be gone a short while, no more than a month."

"Do you have an address for this Colonel Stratton? I'll be happy to phone or send a telegram for you to explain things here. I don't think you'll be leaving for several more days, Miss. We need to

121

make sure you don't develop pneumonia; that's the real danger now."

"Fine, yes, I understand. I really do; I'm a nurse myself. It's just that, well… I'm also supposed to meet a friend, I mean… when the fighting stops he's going to go to the hospital in Brest looking for me and…"

"And you won't be there. That is a shame, but he'll find out you've come back to the States. Surely he'll look for you here?"

"He might not be shipped back for months. There are nearly three million of our boys over there; we'll be occupying Germany and providing relief for refugees. Oh, it's going to be a mess, a real mess. I shouldn't have come home…" Esther began to cry. The nurse patted her on the shoulder and softly assured her that Colonel Stratton would find out where she was.

In her weakened condition, Esther had cried herself back to sleep. She woke again, feeling a bit better, but with no energy at all. A minute later the nurse came back into her room, telling her an hour had passed. Esther asked if she had sent a telegram to the Colonel's office.

"Better than that; I got through on the telephone to the conference location. I don't have good news, I'm sorry to say. You didn't know that the Colonel came down with influenza himself? I'm afraid he died weeks ago; in fact, he was buried at an Army fort yesterday."

"No! I must be dreaming…. it's a nightmare. The poor man; he'd just lost his wife last month. Oh, what am I to do? I have to get back to France, but now with the Colonel…." Esther didn't have the strength to cry again.

"You rest; it's the best thing for you right now. I'll send a telegram to your family in Wisconsin; just give me their address. You'll also need to eat and gain your health back before you even THINK of going to France again."

"I guess you're right. I would like some water, please."

"Of course I'm right….. the nurse is always right, my dear." she said with a smile and a wink.

On the Train

It didn't help that a large part of the first day's trip was across Wisconsin. All Doc could think of was where he'd find Esther; Boston he hoped, but he was prepared to travel to France or beyond to find her. Somehow he'd have to arrange for transport across the sea as a soldier; he didn't have the money to secure passage on a civilian liner. He was careful to not get ahead of himself in thought. One problem at a time was nearly more than he could think about anyway. First was connecting with a train to Boston when this one got to New York. As he rode across the rolling hills past streams and small towns his thoughts drifted a bit toward where he and Esther might live after they reunited. He found it difficult to picture her, with her education and demeanor, living and working at the farm in Oakview. He would suggest they live there until he found other work. But what other work? Hard as he tried, he simply could not think of any other employment there would be if they lived in farm country. Perhaps if they moved to a larger city, like St Paul, Esther could work at a hospital and he could find a job. Doc realized the only training he'd ever really had revolved around a farm... or killing. Well, he'd have to go back to school to learn a new trade. To take his mind off its meandering, he picked up the Minnesota Pioneer newspaper, bought on his way to catching the train. As he read, he was thinking past the words and paragraphs. Realizing how important and powerful knowledge is, he wondered what it would take to operate a printing press.

The miles passed with the soft, rhythmic 'clack-clack' of the rails; a sound that was felt as much as heard. It lulled him to sleep several times during the day as he traveled. The rest did not make up for the loss of the night before, but did serve to clear his thinking a bit. Passing out of Chicago, where there had been a stop for nearly an hour, a long section of the rail line was made up of shorter lengths of track, causing the sound to speed up. Doc had just drifted into another nap when the faster pace turned into the familiar 'put-put-put' of a machine gun. He awoke, startled and breathing hard. Looking around to find no other passenger had noticed him, he realized just how 'on edge' he was feeling. He opened the package he'd bought at the stop in Chicago and took out a chunk of sausage and some cheese, taking alternate bites of each. When he'd finished half he carefully wrapped the rest and put it back into his kit. With his meal for the day complete, Doc opened the Tribune paper he'd found in the station, immediately intrigued by the difference in the type style and weight of the paper itself. Yes, he thought, working as a printer might be quite interesting.

Doc drifted off to sleep again, hoping that it would help the time pass more swiftly. He woke to the sight of huge clouds of smoke off to the north along the horizon. Staring out the window he wondered at how large the fires he was watching must be. Another passenger, sitting two seats ahead of him, spoke up.

"Quite the view; that's what makes our country the greatest in the world. Those mills produce something like 80% of all the steel made. Coal from right here in Pennsylvania fires the furnaces that turn iron ore brought across the Great Lakes from Duluth into the stuff. From here the steel goes all over the world to be made into everything from railroads to razor blades."

The man stood and walked down the aisle to sit next to Doc. He introduced himself as Carl Wickman; traveling to Newark, New Jersey. Wickman explained that he lived in Hibbing, on the edge of the Mesabi Iron Range and was hoping to purchase several large trucks in New Jersey. He planned on having them converted into passenger buses and used to transport workers in the iron ore mines. He'd come from Sweden and began working as a driller in the mines near Hibbing years before. Now he had a vision of building a network of transportation that would be much more flexible that the railroads. He saw people traveling in his buses between cities that didn't even have rails. It would open up whole new places to live and work; a man could have a home outside of the town he worked in, miles away. With his new vehicles he was going to connect Hibbing with several other towns up on "da range" as Carl called the mining area.

Doc marveled at the foresight of the man; how he could look into the future like that. Here he was trying to figure out his own life for the next few days, maybe a couple of weeks at the most and this man was looking years ahead at what his life would be like. The next couple of hours were spent with the two talking about many things, helping to pass the time and the miles. Doc explained to Carl his own trip; how he had to get to Boston quickly to find Esther before she left for France. Carl explained that this was the perfect example of how his buses would be a much better system that the railroads, which were confined to traveling only where the rails were. In a bus, people traveled like in an automobile, going

124

practically wherever they wanted to go, provided there was a road. The real benefit was that roads could be built nearly anywhere, without having to lay down steel rails and wooden ties. Roads could be made out of dirt and gravel; better ones out of asphalt or even cement.

Carl and Doc spoke together with an easy familiarity. At the end of a pleasant afternoon's conversation Carl provided the name and address of a personal friend of his that managed one of the daily newspapers in Minneapolis. He encouraged Doc to get in contact with the friend when he returned to Minnesota. Carl was sure there would be a job for him at his friend's business. Doc thanked him and wished him the best of luck on his plan to expand a bus service in the iron range region.

A porter came into the car announcing that the train would be stopping in fifteen minutes. This was where Doc needed to get off in order to connect with the train that would take him to Boston. As the train approached the station, Doc looked out the window at the sight of a much larger and expanded Fort Upton. He had spent some time at Upton before shipping over to France; that was before the base had grown to its present size. Doc was amazed that so much building could be accomplished in so little time. He saw a large multi-story whitewashed structure and read the sign announcing it as the 'Base Hospital'. In his mind he pictured Esther working in a hospital like that one while he continued with a military career. Shaking his head he let out an audible "No" and realized his days in the Army were drawing to a close. He felt sure that his own future would pivot on an interview in Minneapolis with the friend of a guy he'd just met on this train. For now he had to concentrate on catching the connecting train to Boston and meeting up with the love of his life. In a hundred years Doc would never have guessed that Esther was gazing out the window of her hospital room at the train as it entered the base station.

Doc had only fifteen minutes to catch the express to Boston; plenty of opportunity to stretch tired muscles and grab a bit more food for the overnight trip. There was not enough time to leave the station, however. He settled into a seat just like the one he'd been in for the past day; another twelve or so hours and he'd be in Boston. He planned on being at the ocean liner pier well before Esther would be boarding; Doc felt he'd have plenty of time to find her now. He made himself as comfortable as possible and began to read a New York Times dated November 12th that he had found on a bench in the Fort Upton station. It was his first opportunity to read about the surrender of Germany; both of the other papers had been printed on the 11th, the day of the armistice.

New York Hospital

"Miss Rundquist, my name is Dr Richards. I'm glad to see you're feeling better; I'll be frank and say we've lost far too many patients that were as sick as you've been. What we're now calling the 'Spanish Flu' has swept through the country killing hundreds of thousands in the past several months. Part of the problem has been a lack of coordination between cities, counties and states in restricting travel and, as a result, the spread of the disease. I see it getting worse with all the soldiers that will be coming back now that the war is over. I understand you've been serving in France; is it as bad there?"

"Truthfully, Doctor Richards, I was only treating influenza victims a short time before coming to the States. I received a wire telling me of my own family's crisis with it and came right back. I do know that in the weeks leading up to my return, the Army hospitals all over France were reporting increasing numbers of cases and the mortality rate seemed so high that many of us believed they were in error. Only when I returned to my own hometown did I really get a picture of the scale of it. There were several dozen new graves in the cemetery and the town only has a few hundred people living in it! That was part of what drove me to return to France; knowing I will be needed there desperately."

"You know you'll be needed wherever you end up. I understand your return to France might not happen now; the nurse explained to me the circumstances. I would like you to remain here for another day, just to make sure you're up to traveling again." The doctor looked at the papers in his hands and continued. "Today is the 15th.... if we discharge you tomorrow, you might consider staying a couple of days in New York City before moving on. I've spoken with someone I know that works with transportation; there is a civilian liner departing New York for Cherbourg on the 19th. It will be the first ship not traveling in a convoy; seems the ocean is finally safe from German submarines. If you'd like, we can arrange passage for you; one less thing you'd have to worry about when you leave here."

126

"Thank you Doctor. All of that is very kind and good news as well. I would enjoy a day or so in the City; perhaps pick up a few things I can use after my return to France. You've all been so wonderful providing me such outstanding care. I appreciate it more than I can express."

"Very well. I'll have a clerk begin making the arrangements right away."

When the door closed Esther began figuring out the timetable for her return to Brest and how she might go about finding Doc in France; if he was still in France when she got there. Leaving New York on the 19th would bring her to Europe shortly before the end of November; she wondered how many soldiers would have been sent back to America in the first month since the war ended. Hopefully not the only one she was in love with.

Boston

The next morning, about the time Esther was getting ready to take a commuter train into New York City from Fort Upton, Doc was in a taxi pulling up to the ocean liner pier in Boston harbor. He felt a bit better after washing up at the station when he got off the train. He was about to give the driver a nice tip for getting him there quickly when the cabbie said, "You know, soldier, my kid brother is over in France somewhere. I can't take money from someone who's been through what he's written to me about. Don't worry about the fare; it's on me."

"Hey, thanks. I hope your brother gets home safe and sound."

The cab drove off and Doc looked up at the immense ship tied to the pier. He didn't know how large liners can be; after all, they had boarded the transport to France at night and he'd never even looked back at it when he got off in France. The only ship he'd really seen up close was the fast Navy destroyer he'd been on and that was pretty small compared to this behemoth. Looking around the pier, he spotted the gangway leading up to the boarding area. There were two men standing at the bottom of it; one was in a ship's officer uniform. Doc approached the two and asked if he could check on the status of a passenger to France. The man in the uniform smiled and introduced himself as the ship's Purser, the very man Doc wanted to talk to.

127

"I have a copy of the passenger list; I'll be right back down. You said the name was Esther Rundquist? Wait here; it should only be a few minutes." The man wrote Esther's name on a slip of paper and headed up the gangway. Doc strolled down the pier toward the stern of the ship. He figured it must be nearly 800 feet long and was a good thirty feet up to the main deck railing. He wondered how many passengers a ship this size could hold. He enjoyed the harbor in the morning. The salty air and screeching gulls were not at all like anything he was used to. As he walked his mind wandered over how far he'd travelled and all he'd been through in the past three weeks since he'd left France. Much of it was a blur of frantic activity; the only thing crystal clear was his determination to find Esther. He was sure today was the day; even now he was watching men loading food and other supplies aboard the liner for the departure later in the afternoon. He was so thankful that he'd made it before she left. Doc smiled at how surprised she would be in a few hours when they'd meet.

He looked back toward the gangway, more than a hundred yards away, and saw the Purser coming down it. Doc quickened his pace; his legs were still a bit stiff from sitting in the train for two days. The Purser motioned to come over; he had a ledger book in his hands.

"You said Esther Rundquist? There's no one by that name on our passenger list I'm afraid. Could she be traveling with someone?"

"No sir. She's supposed to be on a ship for France leaving Boston today. This is the only one scheduled? Any chance she's not purchased a ticket yet?"

"This is the only ship. Even with the war over, passenger travel to Europe hasn't picked up enough for more sailings. No other ship is departing for France for the next several days; at least not from Boston. There are no vacancies on today's sailing either; no chance she could still book passage. I'm sorry."

Doc was devastated. All of a sudden he felt so tired and confused; had so counted on this working out perfectly, as he'd hoped. The realization that he had no back up plan came to him; his two weeks of leave had started when he left Fort Snelling three days ago. It wouldn't work to travel back to Minnesota again to visit his folks for a couple of days, only to turn around again and…. no, that would be too much time on a train for anyone. He resigned himself to the hope that the Army would send him back to France; to head down to Fort Upton, report in and see what orders there might be for him. France was where he'd have to find her.

New York City

Esther enjoyed being out in the fresh air again. The train ride was relaxing with its rhythmic motion; she had always enjoyed traveling this way. The subway ride to her hotel was not nearly the same with the hustle and bustle of people. It was a good thing she'd had her luggage sent directly to the hotel from the train depot. She emerged from the underground station and stood for several minutes soaking in the sights; buildings soaring high into the air above her head, threatening to blot out the sky. She was awestruck at the number of people on the sidewalks and the traffic in the streets; trolleys and trucks, automobiles and horse drawn wagons. As she began to walk she could make out at least a dozen different languages all being spoken within earshot. She had fallen in love with Paris years before because of its metropolitan lifestyle; here she was a bit overwhelmed by one difference. In Paris people seemed to take an easy flowing style to life; here everyone was intent on getting somewhere, and soon.

Esther spent a few hours shopping at Bellas Hess & Company on her way to the hotel. Buying an assortment of practical and necessary items, she also allowed herself one new outfit for the voyage to France. She loved the large brimmed hats that were the new style but declined, citing a lack of space to keep it while traveling. In addition, she picked out a beautiful dress that showed off more ankle than had been acceptable before, even in Paris. This one she planned on wearing the first time she and Dautin had dinner when they got together again. Particularly enjoyable was the way her heart fluttered when she put it on and paraded in front of the mirror, imagining the look on his face. The clerk arranged for her purchases to be brought over the next day.

Continuing on to the hotel Esther picked up a theater guide to look at. She planned to take in a Broadway show that evening; something she knew 'one had to do' when in New York City. She was hoping that *The Pirates of Penzance* was showing; though not a new musical, she had wanted to see it for years. Esther sighed at the thought of going alone and looked forward to the happy day when she and Doc would be together to enjoy such outings. Checking into the hotel took moments and she was soon in her room; nothing grand but it did have a comfortable bed and private bath. Taking her time, Esther enjoyed a long warm soak in the tub and a much needed rest before dressing for dinner in the hotel's restaurant.

Boston

Doc, too, enjoyed a long warm soak. He'd decided to get a room in Boston before heading by train down to Fort Upton. He still had plenty of furlough time left, though he didn't want to wait too long before setting off to Europe. The local newspaper didn't mention anything about troops returning to the States; perhaps he'd be lucky and get transport back to his unit before the Army's recall began. He would know in a day or so; the ticket in his pocket was for a morning train. He'd arrive at Upton in the evening and would check in from leave then. Meanwhile, the hot water in the tub was calling his name and he didn't want to disappoint...

The next morning Doc ate a large breakfast in the hotel, having the restaurant pack him a lunch for the trip as well. A short cab ride and he was on the train relaxing, reading a paper when he started on his way south. The good night sleep, coupled with the wonderfully hot bath, had helped him to think and relax a little. He felt secure that, even if the Army couldn't get him to France, he'd be able to travel on his own. He had telegraphed home from the hotel and asked his father to wire him enough money for the trip, knowing his folks were aware of his mission to find Esther since his letter from Fort Snelling would have been received by now. The funds should arrive at Fort Upton in a few days; by then he'd know how he would sail. It was either in a troopship, jammed in like sardines in a can, or as a passenger on a liner similar to the one in Boston. He was beginning to hope the Army would not accommodate him....

When he reached Fort Upton, Doc reported to the Administration Building. He was informed by the duty officer that he could spend the night in a visitor's room and report for assignment first thing in the morning. Doc put his kit in the room and wandered around the base, stretching his legs, before heading to the NCO Club for a beer; maybe two. The duty officer was not aware of any units preparing to ship over to France and had actually given Doc a rather strange look when asked about it. While in the Club, Doc was on the receiving end of several drinks, compliments of soldiers at the Fort; most of whom were patently relieved that they would not be sent into fighting in France. They enjoyed hearing his stories from the front lines; most of these new Sergeants had never fired a weapon in anger at all. To sit with one who had been presented three Croix de Guerre's and buy him a beer was as close to combat as most hoped to get. They especially liked his two headed coin, the gift from Digger. By the time the Club closed, Doc wasn't exactly sure of the way to his room; he was guided by a somewhat raucous group of doughboys, all with stripes on.

Oakview

Jack was at Fedder's store when the telegram came in. After reading it he walked across the street to the Farmer's Bank and arranged for enough funds to be wired to Dautin in New York. He left thinking about the ability to send money across the continent in a few hours and how life was changing as time went by. When he got back to the farm Phebe was reading Doc's letter, again.

"I'm still trying to understand just what that boy is attempting to do. Going all the way to Boston to try and stop Esther from sailing back to France? What does he plan to do if she agrees? Has he asked her father for permission to court her, let alone marry the girl? No. Has he given us the opportunity to even meet her? No. Heavens, sometimes I wonder about Weldon boys, even my own."

"All in good time, dear. Sometimes action is what's called for. I'm sure you've raised him to not go completely overboard; once he finds her, he's sure to do things right. I know we're not all the perfect gentlemen we ought to be. I recall some who have even split their trousers to attract attention." His smile was meant to diffuse her frustration; it worked like a charm.

Phebe laughed at him. Jack hugged her and said the things she wanted to hear; that her son loved her and would do the right things. Mostly though, he told her that he loved her and only wanted to do the right things as well. He then mentioned the telegram he'd received while in town and the action he felt was important enough to take without having the chance to speak together first. It was masterfully done; Phebe agreed with Jack, even though it was quite a sum of money. His next suggestion was received a little differently.

131

"Now? I've got bread in the oven and you've got chores to do Mister Weldon! You're going to have to work a bit harder to bring in the money you just gave away to that son of ours." As she said this, hands on hips, Phebe posed with a scornful look on her face. Jack started for the door like a whipped puppy, turned and saw Phebe smiling.

"The bread will be done in twenty minutes. Be back in here in half an hour; and be sure to wash up first."

New York City

Esther had not enjoyed the show as she had hoped, feeling alone in a sea of couples. Even at intermission it seemed everybody at the theater was with someone. When the show ended, she quickly exited, hailing a cab to bring her back to the hotel where she headed up to her room. The tears followed closely the shutting of the door. She seemed to miss Doc more and more; really felt they were an ocean apart. Recognizing the metaphor, she stopped crying. Esther knew she would not stay and work at the hospital in Brest until she had found him. That had to happen first; then her duties as a nurse could resume. In two days she'd be on the ship to France with plenty of time to think and plan a strategy for finding him. In the meantime she needed to rest; the evening out had exhausted her.

Fort Upton

He woke at first light with two overwhelming desires; the first was to empty his bladder, then he would start the next phase of Operation Esther. Doc's head was still a bit fuzzy when he reported to the Admin Building after chow. The food, though welcome, was sitting a bit heavy in his stomach; welcoming him back to the Army. He was trying to organize his thoughts and focus on what today's plan of action was when the duty officer motioned him into an office.

"Sergeant Weldon, I'm Captain Adams. I understand you're looking for a ride back to France to rejoin your unit? Admirable, but I don't see how that would be possible at present. A directive came in just last evening instructing the Fort to begin preparations to receive the first of our men coming back from Europe. With the war over, the country needs to demobilize; war is expensive. We're actually expecting the first contingents to arrive the beginning of next week. I don't see how you're going to get back there anytime soon. I could put you to work here or you can use the remainder of your furlough. Let's see, that would be another five days. Why don't you take a few of those days, see New York and check back? We may have more information to help you by then."

"Thanks, Captain. It's more than wanting to get back to my unit though. You see sir, there's this girl, a nurse in Brest..."

"I appreciate the honesty, Sergeant. I really don't think the Army would prioritize that over you returning to your duty. Give me a couple of days to look into what might be done, alright?"

"Yes sir. Any chance of my getting an extension to my furlough if I book passage on a civilian liner at my own expense? I am prepared to do that, sir. I really aim to get to France if I have to swim there."

"I guess you do. I'm not sure about the furlough; not exactly textbook thinking for an enlisted man. Can you wait one day? I'll look into this and have an answer for you tomorrow."

"Thank you Captain. I'll be back in tomorrow morning. Maybe a day in New York would do me good; I can find out about passage and ship schedules."

"Great idea. I know two Corporals that come from the city; would you care to take them with you for the day, kind of guide you around? It's a big city, easy to get lost."

"I remember how large it is from my first time here. That would help, sir. Thanks again."

"I'll have the two meet you at your quarters in half an hour and see you tomorrow. Good luck, Sergeant."

Doc was a bit disappointed, but he couldn't expect the Army to put a ship at his disposal to help him find his girl. Maybe if he was a General or something; certainly not a dog faced Sergeant. He was glad the Captain had offered a couple of men to help him find his way around New York; he remembered his trip to see the Giants baseball team with Digger and how confusing it could be to get around. He walked back to his room to wait for the two men.

New York City

Esther slept until nearly eight o'clock; she'd have to take it a bit easier today. She realized how much the sickness had taken from her. She would be wise to rest more often, especially with her departure for France only two days away. Today she would simply do a last bit of shopping and then come back to her room to begin packing for France. First though would be a bite to eat; she was quite hungry and considered it a good sign that she was well on her way back to full health. She bathed, got dressed and headed down to the hotel restaurant.

Doc and his two companions had spent the hour ride into the city getting to know one another. The Corporals had both come from New York, though from different boroughs. The way they talked about home, Doc would have guessed they lived states apart. He could only laugh when they began to compare baseball teams; one liked the Dodgers, the other a 'dyed in the wool' Yankees follower. Doc was glad he wasn't an ardent Giants fan or they'd never agree on anything. The three took a subway down to the waterfront area to check into available passage to France; Doc found out a ship was leaving in two days and still had a few cabins. He didn't reserve one right away, still hoping the Army would find a way to get him there. The clerk assured Doc that he would set aside a reservation for him until tomorrow.

That part of their mission accomplished, they all agreed it was a good time to grab some chow. Corporal Evans, the Dodgers fan, said he had a cousin that worked in a restaurant not far from where they were. He assured the others they could get a great meal at a cheap price. It was best to go 'Dutch treat' as Evans put it, each paying his own way, in light of what the two Corporals had heard about Doc's special flipping coin. They both wanted to take a look at it, however. As soldiers do, the three soon turned their conversation to the subject of girls.

"Let me get this straight. You looked into booking passage to France, out of your own pocket, so you can find a dame?" Evans said in disbelief.

The other Corporal, Connors, was a bit more understanding. He had his own girl over on 'the Joysie side' as he put it. He thought Doc was wise in letting Captain Adams help him out; he'd known the Captain before the Army and said he was 'a smahhht guy'.

That started a block long argument between the two about their CO's merits. Doc could understand most of what they said but felt an interpreter would be handy.

"Here we are; the restaurant's inside." Evans walked up the steps leading into the building.

Esther had finished a wonderful breakfast and was walking through the lobby. She would have the doorman get her a cab outside and waited as two soldiers came through the door. As she entered the revolving door she glanced up to see another soldier going in. Their eyes locked....

Evans and Connor had never seen two people have so much trouble getting out of a door. Weldon and some dame seemed to go around and around, trying to both exit in or outside. The doughboys stood laughing when Doc finally followed the girl into the lobby of the hotel. When the two embraced in a passionate kiss, Evans was first to speak up.

"Boy, some guys have the luck."

"And he thinks he has to go all the way to France to find a dame?" Connors answered.

Doc, Esther and the two New Yorkers went into the restaurant and sat down. While Evans and Connor ate a meal, Doc and Esther recounted their adventures since leaving Europe, tucked away in a private booth.

Doc said goodbye to Connors and Evans and asked them to let the Captain know he'd still be back at Fort Upton in the morning. He booked a room for himself before taking Esther to Central Park, a place both wanted to visit. While sitting in the sunshine of a cool November afternoon the two talked of their future together. Their first decision was that neither had to go back to Europe; Esther would cancel her booking from the hotel. With golden leaves falling like rain around them, carried along with the autumn breeze, Dautin asked Esther to marry him; on the condition that her father gave his consent when they visited him on their way to Oakview. Esther happily said "Yes" on the condition that his parents also agreed when they arrived at the farm. As the sun was setting they returned to the hotel for dinner. The meal was delicious, though a desire to continue holding hands made eating difficult. After a short walk on the streets of nighttime New York they parted company at Esther's door after a loving kiss. Both slept better than either had in a long time.

In the morning Esther was up, dressed and at Doc's door before he was ready. He let her in as he finished putting on his uniform.

"It will seem strange to have you see me in anything other than one of these" he said as he buttoned his tunic. "I mean, besides the pajamas I had to wear in the hospital."

"I suppose a confession is in order. As your nurse, there were moments.... ahh, before you were conscious that required me to... you know. I mean, you had to be cleaned up and your wounds dressed and, well... I do believe you're blushing, Sergeant Weldon."

"I'd never thought of that. I guess you'll have one thing up on me, for awhile at least." Doc smiled and gave Esther a hug. "Now, let's go see what we can talk the Army into; or out of."

"After we eat downstairs, my love. I cannot say I've missed Army food in any shape or way they serve it. Hospital food in France was bad enough, I won't face what they have here."

"Yes, ma'am; whatever you say." Doc gave her a silly salute as they walked down the hallway to the lift.

They arrived at Fort Upton shortly before noon and immediately checked in to the Admin Office. Captain Adams was sent for and arrived after a few minutes. He smiled as he saw Doc and Esther arm in arm.

"Good morning, Sergeant. Corporal Evans reported to me last evening; I'll take liberty and say, Miss, that I understand Weldon's willingness to swim across the Atlantic to find you."

"Why thank you, Captain. That's most kind. I'm glad you were here to help. It's strange to think we might have actually run into each other on the ship going back to Europe. How different that would have been."

"Indeed. I do have news for you, too, Sergeant. It happens your squad will be aboard the ship arriving on Monday. Apparently someone decided that the first to get to France should be the first home as well. If you'd like, I can arrange for you to join them on their return to Fort Snelling for discharge. Those that want to get back to civilian life will be given the opportunity when they return there. Might I assume you'll be one making that decision, too?"

"Yes, sir, I will. There's something we'll be doing shortly after my discharge. This is working out better than I could have dreamed. Esther, how about we ask Digger to be our Best Man? I know you've never met him, but he's a swell guy. I'm sure we can talk him into it."

"That would be wonderful, dear. I'll be asking my sister to be Maid of Honor, so.."

Captain Adams chuckled and broke in, "Well, I'll leave you two to find the Planning Division Office; looks like you'll be there awhile. In the mean time, I've extended your furlough for two additional days so you won't have to return until Monday when the ship arrives. Be here by Zero-900 hours, Sergeant."

"Yes, sir; I won't be a minute late. I mean, WE won't be a minute late, sir."

Oakview

They read the telegram from Dautin together, on the way into the house after getting it from Roscoe. Phebe laughed; tears of joy on her cheeks brought an almost forgotten feeling of happiness.

"He found her in New York? That will be a story I want to hear. Coming home in a week with Esther and the rest of his unit? How many people is that with Esther's father and sister? Must be more than two dozen! Heavens, Jack! We've got work to do.... we can put the soldiers in the barn; they'll be used to that. Let's see... Esther and her sister in the boys' room, her father in our room, we can sleep in the living room... what about Dautin?"

"Oh, he'll be fine on the roof, I'm sure, dear. Honestly, let's have a cup of coffee and figure this all out. We still have time before the madness starts."

"Said just like a man" Phebe teased.

On the Train Home

"Listen up… quiet you guys." Digger was working hard to get everyone's attention. The soldiers that filled the car were all well known to Doc, who was trying to introduce Esther. "OK, that's better. Esther, let me do this. Doc's been out of action far too long. Alright, Esther…. this is Cook, Duggan, Thompson, Walters, Anderson, oh, what the hell am I doing? I can hardly remember all their names and I've been with them near on two years!"

"Nice try, Digger. I'll take the time we have on this ride to get to know each, I'm sure. I certainly feel safe with an entire car full of men as my personal bodyguard and escort." Esther knew the whole event would be grand, and memorable. She and Doc had spent the days before the troop ship pulled in making arrangements for her father, sister and the men of the squad to meet at Oakview for a wedding. Thankfully, telephones and telegraph made it all come together in such a short time. The only question she and Doc hadn't answered yet was where they would live after they became husband and wife.

"You know, love. If we lived in Wisconsin I'm sure my father could arrange for you to find work. He does know several contractors who will be looking for help."

"Darling, I'm not sure I want to work construction. I met a man on my way to finding you that has a friend in Minneapolis who owns a newspaper. I've given a lot of thought about learning a trade like printing. And there's a fine, large hospital nearby as well."

"Well, it seems we can live in either state. Father's best friend also owns a chain of newspapers. If you'd like to be a printer, I'm sure he could be of help. As I see it the decision may be a simple one of location. But how do we choose?"

Doc answered right up. "Hey, how about we flip a coin? I happen to have one right here…" as he reached into his pocket.

"Wait, wait a minute", piped in Digger. "Esther, I have a lucky coin right here. Why don't you use this one and call heads on the way up?" As he tossed it up, Doc looked at his best friend and said, "Did your brother send you another one?"

The coin went up, end over end. Esther called out "Heads" as all of the men started to laugh. The coin hit the floor and stuck, caught edgewise between two cracks.

Esther looked at it and said, with a smile, "Well, boys; I guess that's one decision we'll make later." She picked the coin out of the crack and put it in her pocket, safe and secure.

Epilogue

Dautin and Esther were married on the farm at Oakview, attended by family and friends. Several members of the squad were also there. Esther wore her mother's wedding ring, a gift from her father. After the wedding Dautin obtained a position with a Minneapolis newspaper working as a printer; a career that spanned many years. He and Esther lived in a town on the edge of the city called St Louis Park, or just "The Park", where they raised two boys, Dale and Don.

Jack and Phebe respected Dautin's decision to move from Oakview, knowing it would leave them shorthanded on the farm. Two of the younger men from Doc's squad came to work as hired hands after their discharge from the Army. Digger chose to remain in the Army; he was killed in Nicaragua in 1926.

America returned to a peace and economic boom that lasted through the 'Roaring 20's'. With a worldwide financial collapse and the subsequent Great Depression, several nations chose leaders that promised growth, security and prosperity… a generation after the First World War the planet was engulfed in a second, even more destructive one.

Dale Weldon would also learn what war can be. Read his own story in Colors in the Air….

Made in the USA
Middletown, DE
24 September 2017